THE WORM THAT WASN'T

Frozen to the ladder, they heard the sounds of voices coming nearer. They both peered upwards, expecting to see the face of Krillan or one of his guards at any moment.

Two eyes appeared at the top of the well. Two bright green eyes. Gim shrieked and dropped to the floor.

It was the worm. The worm was slithering down towards them, no doubt moving away from Krillan and his men.

Leah jumped down to him.

"They've spooked it. Come on, move it!"

The two of them ran blindly now, trying not to hit their heads on the roof of the tunnel.

Behind them, in the dark, the worm cast a rueful eye upward at the sky above it, thwarted by the soldiers. But smelling their scent, it licked the walls and floor and, with a crafty, purposeful slither, it followed Leah and Gim down the tunnel.

An Abaddon Books™ Publication
www.abaddonbooks.com
abaddon@rebellion.co.uk

First published in 2008 by Abaddon Books™, Rebellion Intellectual
Property Limited, The Studio, Brewer Street, Oxford, OX1 1QN, UK.

10 9 8 7 6 5 4 3 2 1

Editor: Jonathan Oliver
Cover: Mark Harrison
Design: Simon Parr & Luke Preece
Marketing and PR: Keith Richardson
Creative Director and CEO: Jason Kingsley
Chief Technical Officer: Chris Kingsley
Dreams of Inan™ created by Andy Boot

ISBN 978-1-905437-53-5

Printed in Denmark by Nørhaven Paperback A/S

DREAMS OF INAN

THE WORM
THAT WASN'T

Mike Maddox

Abaddon
Books

WWW.ABADDONBOOKS.COM

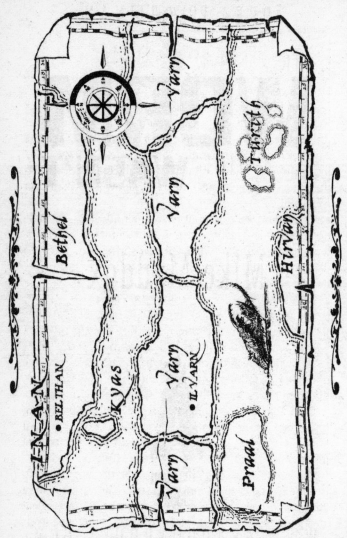

PROLOGUE

The last days of the Great War

The sunset had been glorious.

From yellow to gold to deep red, the sun had sunk slowly behind the hills, casting a rich amber glow over the fields and woods. It had been a warm day, and the sudden drop in temperature only made it all the more beautiful. The smells of the land changed as the heat left the fields. Subtler scents now overshadowed by the richer smells of earth.

The sky turned from a deep summer blue, to dark blue, to darker blue. The final rays of the sun turned the clouds on the horizon into bright red fields of colour. After the heat of the day, night was a relief. It caressed all the senses at once as the final glow vanished.

It was then that the screaming started.

The military attack ships dropped in from high altitude. They fell through the tracer fire like cherry blossoms blown on the wind, bringing death in their wake. There was something beautifully serious about them. Like thoughts of murder and suffering given physical form, they fell with a sound like razor wire on sheet metal.

Gold Company had dug in well, but had been expecting the attack to come from the expanse of no mans land that lay in front of them. The aircraft had come from their exposed left flank, taking them off guard.

The soldiers trained their guns on the enemy craft, struggling with their bulky armour. The aircraft were brutal and inelegant in design and packed with magical defences, making them hard to focus on. Looking at one was like trying to remember a dream, or trying to understand a complicated idea; all this while people around you were shooting or dying.

Captain Niaal ducked as one of the ships whistled overhead, showering the ground with silver darts. The trench had shelters, but they were a hundred yards down the line. The soldiers would be dead before they could get there. Pressing himself into the side of the trench Niaal pulled his night vision goggles down fast, feeling the familiar sense of déjà vu and fear as the night sky burned into visible red.

"How many sir? I count three." his Lieutenant, Carleaf, said, weapon pushed hard to his shoulder, scanning the dark skies. "Bloody things. We should have had warning. What the ninth hell is early warning up to anyway?"

Niaal's brow furrowed. "Four. Three ahead, one behind. Looks a different design to others. Possibly a freighter."

Carleaf pointed up. "There, sir. Directly overhead. It's hovering. Listing to starboard, looks like it's in trouble."

Niaal knew this might be their best chance. The attack ships were too fast to draw a bead on anyway, but a lumbering freighter caught from beneath was a target they could hope to hit. "Carleaf! Bolt gun party! At the double!"

Three men came puffing down the trench, bringing the heavy weapon with them. "Straight up lads, we'll only get one shot at this."

The soldiers fell to the job like cogs in a machine. It was the thing they had trained for over and over again, until they could do it with their eyes closed. Until they could do it in their sleep if need be. Most of all they could do it quietly, quickly and with no messing about. As soon as the base plate was slapped down, the legs were in place and the gun slotted in position. The hell with regulations, they pulled their gloves off with their teeth to spin the flywheels and locking nuts into place. Dropping to their knees, they aimed the gun straight up to where the ship bobbed uncertainly in the breeze.

"Captain! The attack ships, they're coming back!"

"Covering fire! They'll be trying to defend the freighter. Hold them off until we can bring the gun to bear!

"Sir. Squad, front, covering fire!"

Niaal looked up. The freighter was moving away. Another minute and it would be beyond their range. "Come on lads, hurry it up!"

The gunner eyed the target, pausing to wipe the sweat from his eyes. "Almost there sir." He stroked the safety catch on the trigger mechanism, feeling the embossed sigils glow with anticipation. His number two slapped him on the shoulder, signalling that the charge was in place. "Gun loaded, awaiting orders to fire!"

There was an explosion fifty feet to the left. The three incoming attack craft had opened fire on their position. The men responded with tracer, dissecting the night with streaks of magnesium coated death.

"Fire!" shouted Niaal. The gun kicked, and spat a flower of destruction into the air. The freighter was caught direct amidships and dissolved into plasma and magic. Indistinct shapes blossomed outwards, as ideas and men rained down. "Direct hit! Well done, boys."

Turning his gaze from the freighter, Niaal now concentrated on the three attack ships, which had turned tail and were now heading for the hills at full speed. Which was strange. The loss of the freighter was a blow to them. Presumably they had been its escort, here to protect it. With the freighter destroyed there was probably no need for them to risk themselves further. But Niaal's men were still sitting targets, and should have been easy enough prey for three ships in formation. Why were they running? It didn't make sense.

"Lieutenant, get a trace on those ships would you?" Carleaf stroked the air in front of him, calling up thought forms showing the field of battle. Three triangular shapes were bobbing away towards the north. "What are they doing?"

"They're running for it, sir. We must have scared them off."

"No. No, that's extremely unlikely. They can see how thin on the ground we are. They would have been safe enough as long as they kept out of the way of the bolt gun."

"Well something's spooked them, sir."

Niaal stood up, looking at the debris that had fallen from the freighter. Slops of plasma sank into the soil from the wreckage of the ship. Pieces of machinery and the bodies of the crew were scattered across their trench. Looking up, Niaal saw what looked like a fine mist falling gently from the sky. At first he thought it was snow, but that was impossible. A piece landed on his sleeve. It was a fibre, a thread the thickness of a fingernail. "That's odd," he said, suddenly alarmed.

"What is, sir?"

"It moved. Look, it's moving." He peered closer. Now Carleaf was leaning in too, to see the strange stuff drifting down around them.

"Perhaps that's what scared the fighters off sir" laughed Carleaf. "Perhaps they're scared of worms. Pilots are soft like that"

"Maybe they were. Maybe they should be."

Niaal pulled his water bottle from his belt, emptied it, and flicked the tiny creature inside with his gloved finger. "But maybe they had very good cause to be. It's probably nothing, but we should take no chances. Sergeant? Tell the men masks down, I want the area sterilised."

"Masks down, we're cooking up. Link in squares and brace for impact!"

The men dropped their visors and instantly sat in circles of eight; arms linked together, heads down, bodies braced. Niaal swung his backpack round, and opened it, withdrawing a blue metal cylinder the size of a water jug. "Ready?" He turned to Carleaf.

"Ready sir."

"Five seconds, four, three –" The two of them linked arms and dropped to the ground, heads down, visors sealed.

For three miles in every direction everything went white. It was suddenly daylight. Every living thing in the air or in the soil tensed and died. Only the soldiers, safe in their suits survived, holding on to one another, eyes screwed tight against the migraine intense pain that briefly shot through them.

They had survived. They had seen them off.

The war was nearly over; the great powers of Inan had seen that the end was in sight and were even now jostling to make sure that each nation came out of the conflict as best they could. In the northern hemisphere, small independent nation states were splintering off from the political giant known as the continent of Bethel. Lesser wizards and generals had risen up, some daring to challenge the might of the great powers of Inan. The Allesh Free State, to whom Niaal and Griggo owed their allegiance, was one such small country. However, they differed from many of the fledgling countries in that they were rallied around a Mage, an incredibly powerful wizard, more usually associated with one of the larger countries. The sheer threat of his power looked almost certain to guarantee that Allesh's enemies would leave them well alone.

Niaal was first back on his toes. "Squad, on your feet. We don't want to get caught like that again. Eyes open, mouths shut, weapons on safety. Sergeant, lead the way."

Niall felt a strange movement under his glove. A sort of tickle. Pulling off his glove he saw that the fingernail of the digit he had flicked the tiny worm with was long, in need of cutting. This would not be a point to be noticed, except that Niaal had cut his nails only that very morning. And yet the nail was now showing a week's growth.

Deciding against clipping his water bottle back on to his belt, he wrapped it in magically reflective material and dropped it into his backpack. If the creature was magical then it made sense to insulate the bottle until he had a better chance to examine it. Setting off, Niaal was at that moment unaware that he had potentially doomed thousands of people to certain death. Safe in the bottle the tiny creature squirmed and wriggled. It knew nothing but blackness.

Blackness and hunger.

The three aircraft regrouped fifty miles north in secure airspace. The mission specialist passengers checked their readings and consulted with headquarters. Three hundred thousand individual worm specimens had been released when the enemy missile struck the decoy freighter. The passengers on board the aircraft opened their minds, allowing themselves to be used as conduits by the fierce, terrible intelligence they worshipped as their master, the Warlord of Varn. They felt him flow through them, felt a thrill of excitement as he brushed aside every memory and every experience they had accumulated over a whole lifetime of service to him, as if they were insects on his robes. The pilots flushed with a terrible dark pride that they were being used so casually.

As their minds reached out and joined with their master, they felt their own consciousnesses expanding. They were able to track the path of individual beads of sweat running down the brows of their enemies below. If they had so wished, they could have mapped the surface of raindrops as one might oceans across some undiscovered continent.

They scoured the battlefield behind them, searching the air, the mud, and the dust. The mind, when they found it, was so tiny it could hardly be called a mind at all. It was animal, obviously, but so primitive, so wild. It had only one thought right now. To feed. To feed and stop the hunger that consumed it.

The joined minds felt their own elation matched and swamped by that of their master.

Despite the sterilisation device, the readings confirmed their hopes. Against all the odds, the mission had succeeded. One specimen had been picked up by the enemy and was even now being transported safely into the very heart of their enemy's territory. Now they need only wait for the worm to do its work, and let the province of Allesh, and all Bethel along with it, starve itself to death.

Pleased with the way the day had gone, the great mind withdrew from his hosts roughly. They slumped in their seats, spent, eyes vacant. It would take several months of intense therapy before they would even be able to control their own bowels again, let alone speak of their experience. But as they lay there in the hospital wards, speechless, unable to even feed themselves, they would be revered as heroes. Nurses back in Varn would wash their faces with grateful tears; men would name their baby sons after them, for what they had done today.

They had won a great victory. If they ever recovered, their lives would be full of honour and gratitude. Far away, their master felt a twitch at the edge of his dreaming, like a sleeping man disturbed by a breeze, and he knew their scheme had prospered. He turned his gaze elsewhere, satisfied that his pawns had done well, like clever ants in a maze. It would be morning soon, the start of a new day, and the start of a new world.

And the end of the old one.

CHAPTER ONE

Fifteen Years Later

There was something wrong with the sky that morning. The colour of the sun, the way the windows of the Castle reflected the dim, cold red light; it was all wrong.

Leah Carleaf stood on the balcony, plaiting her auburn hair, a ribbon held in her mouth. She wasn't sure what it was exactly that was wrong with the sky. Something about the colours, the shape of the clouds. She couldn't point to it, but it was there in front of her, a niggling annoyance to early morning eyes, bleary and still far more asleep than awake.

"Leah!" A clear musical voice cut through her daydream. Saran, her mother, called from the kitchen below. "Your breakfast is going cold! You'll be late for work again."

"I'll be right down." Leah called back.

Like all workers in the Garden, Leah wore the simple peasant dress of country folk, albeit with a synthetic fabric that repelled the dirt and dust. Just one of the many blessings from the Mage.

Sliding her feet into her slippers she peered down at the street below, which was now starting to fill with market traders setting up their stalls and trades-people hurrying by on their way to work. Some of them were talking and bidding each other a good morning, others silent, still munching food as they hurried along deep in thought.

Her father had never been late for work.

The thought of him caught her unawares, a sudden dull pain inside. He had always been the first out of bed; the first to get the fire going in the kitchen, bringing her hot honey drinks in the winter, or playing with her in the warm early summer mornings before school.

Leah's father, Griggo Carleaf, was a hero of the last Great War. The conflict had lasted five hundred years, and had all but destroyed the world of Inan. Entire generations grew knowing nothing but fire and violence. Griggo had fought for the army that followed the wizard known as the Mage Pillian, creating the new independent nation of Allesh. The war over, he had returned to his academic studies as head botanist in the Garden, the magical powerhouse of the Protectorate.

But the Mage had no appetite for government, and had built himself a castle, a magical construct where he could lose himself in meditation and study. He created the role of Sages, lesser magic users and scientists, whom he chose to rule the lands in his name. The Sages in turn surrounded themselves with Chemical Warriors, troops well versed in magic, who would serve them in all things.

Although the Mages of Inan possessed the power to create magical weapons of mass destruction, Pillian had been a minor player in the great game of war and empire. Above all else, he loved plants, and the magical properties they possessed. And so it was he created the Gardens of Allesh, in the hope that in studying nature, he might find a way to heal the planet, which had been so violated by war.

"Leah! Breakfast!" It was her mother's voice again, louder, more insistent. Leah threw her warmest cloak over her shoulders and ran down the narrow staircase, following the smell all the way to the kitchen table.

"Do my hair for me?" she asked as she sat down.

Saran sighed. "Honestly, you must learn to go to bed earlier, this is getting ridiculous. You'll be losing your job if you carry on like this," she said, twisting Leah's hair into braids. "And we need the money."

"But if I don't study then I'll be stuck in this same position forever!" blurted Leah, her mouth full of bread. "And if I don't study then there's no point even taking my exams, is there?"

"I thought you liked your job."

"I do. I – ow!"

"Sorry."

"I just want to do more with my life than be a Gardener." Leah caught her mother's expression, suddenly sharp, in the mirror across the room. "Of course, there's nothing wrong with being a Gardener."

"It was good enough for your father."

"And it's a good enough job for me, I know that. If it weren't for the Gardens, then the Sages would have nothing to work with. Without us, without the Chemists, we'd be defenceless. I know all this." Leah sighed. "We are part of the same army, we all are needed; all parts work together." she said in a dull, flat voice, reciting the credo learned by all children at school.

"All parts work together," chorused Saran, finishing her hair. "There." She stepped back, smiling.

"What?" Leah said, over the top of her goblet.

"Just admiring my handiwork."

"Really?" Leah said, glancing in the mirror over the fireplace. "My hair looks the same as always."

"I wasn't talking about your hair."

Leah jumped to her feet and gave Saran a hug. "Love you," she said, her mouth full of seed bread again.

"And I love you. But you need to start acting like an adult, Leah. I know you're clever, they know you're clever, but if you're not there on time what does it matter!"

Blowing her mother a kiss, Leah ran to the door, remembering to pick up her data phial from the dish on the dresser. Pulling the door to the cottage closed behind her she stepped lightly out onto the street and into a whole new day. Which would probably be exactly like yesterday unless she managed to get through the exams which were waiting for her.

Sliding the phial into her wrist-port she felt the sudden data rush, as updates from work, her friends, the usual threats and rumours of war, flickered across her eyes, before settling down into her core memory.

She shook her head, shivering. Her good mood, all of one hour old, paused, spun around and fled as the news sank in. Another death in the village, the third in as many weeks. The same as before, the same sickness. The Sages in the Castle were supposed to be working on a cure, but as yet there was none to be found. For the past two weeks, the illness had been the talk of every inn, schoolyard and workplace. Allesh was a small country and bad news travelled fast.

This was why her work was important. Without the raw materials provided by the Garden, the Sages would have nothing to work with. Lacking the tools to do the job the Mage employed them for, the illness might spread unchecked. Her mother was right. It was time to grow up

Although the world of Inan was technically in a state of peace, the fallout from five centuries of conflict was still ongoing, with many newly created republics and kingdoms still flexing their muscles in relation to each other. Allesh was one such country, nestled in the western corner of the continent of Bethel. It had a large port, which served as a commercial hub for traders between Bethel and Varn, the huge land far across the seas to the south. It was mostly farmland, and home to a generally peaceful people, glad to see the back of the war, and generally hopeful for what the future might hold.

The sound of stamping feet and hooves broke her thoughts as rapidly as the bad news had but a second before. Leah stood to one side of the narrow cobbled street as, around the corner, the unmistakable sight of the militia came tramping into view, the clanking of their brown armour echoing off the walls.

"Make way! Make way for the militia! Official business," called the herald, riding alongside Captain Krillan at the head of the column. The militia, local men all, winked and smiled at their friends and neighbours as they made their way towards the market square. These were not professional soldiers but volunteers, farmers, builders; ordinary people helping out in difficult times.

Krillan was from The Castle, sent to lead the militia only last year. He had made it abundantly clear that he felt the job beneath him, and this was reflected not only in his manners, but in outward expressions such as his uniform. Although the same colour as the earthy brown all militiamen wore, his was the shape and cut of a front line cavalry officer. He was not, it was fair to say, greatly liked. And, as Leah knew only too well, this didn't seem to bother him greatly.

Krillan sat bolt upright on his horse, neither noticing nor acknowledging those beneath him. His gaze was, or so he thought, distant and noble. His eyes, or so he thought, were set on far better things. This was, or so Leah had decided long ago, because his head was stuck firmly up his arse.

Leading the militia would never be enough for Krillan, thought Leah. Even if his men won a war single handed, his face would still burn with the shame of being asked to lead peasants instead of regular soldiers.

As the troop passed by, the data phial in Leah's wrist

suddenly burned with a scratching sensation. Many people with skin as sensitive as hers occasionally suffered a reaction to the implant. She snatched her hand up to her face, rubbing the soreness with her fingers.

Krillan's horse, face-to-face with her, took fright and sidestepped, causing him to lurch in the saddle. Krillan glared at her. To Leah it was as if he was furious that he had to even soil his gaze with the lower classes.

The troop came to an abrupt halt behind him, men bumping into each other clumsily.

Leah looked up at the officer, suddenly afraid to be held by such a steady gaze.

"Madam, you seem distressed. May we assist you?" Krillan's words were politeness personified but hissed with such arrogance, such venom.

"My wrist implant. It burned me."

"Most unfortunate. You may wish to have it seen to." Krillan's eyes were already on the horizon again. "Good morning."

With a shout from the Herald, the militia set off once more down the narrow cobbled street. A few raised their eyebrows at Leah as they passed, tutting and shaking their heads in amusement.

"Sorry!" called Leah after them. A smile slowly dawning across her face. "Mind you, I thought a war horse would be made of sterner stuff myself," she smirked. "Scared by girls. What's it going to do if it has to fight a battle?" She looked up at the Castle. "A real one."

The Castle overshadowed everything. Not just the village but, figuratively and politically speaking, all the land immediately to the east and south. The neighbouring country of Prash-Romaria had been Allesh's ally in the Great War. Like Allesh, they were formerly part of Greater Bethel, and subject to will of the Mage Ramus-Bey. But the two had drifted apart along cultural and religious lines in the recent past. Once the war had ended, their differences seemed suddenly larger than the things that had once held them in common. Although they lacked the magical firepower of a Mage, the Prash-Romarians had enough skilled wizards to keep their borders safe. Bethel tolerated these smaller breakaway countries, as long as they kept themselves to themselves, and as long as they were satisfied that the Alleshi Mage Pillian was content to lose himself in his books rather than play empire builder.

It would be an understatement to call Pillian's Castle 'big'. It was, in all fairness, enormous. The walls were aquamarine, lit from within by shifting lights that seemed to come from everywhere and yet nowhere. No flags or pennants flew over the towers, but there was a constant heat haze, a blurring of the air not from fire or furnace, but from thought and magic and something else; something very like madness. It was at once both beautiful and terrible. Leah had known it her whole her life, and like everyone else in the village, she wavered between never noticing it at all and being constantly struck in awe at the enormous majesty of it.

The Castle was not 'real' in any meaningful sense. It was there, it existed, but it was something so complicated, so wonderful that it went beyond mere reality. As Leah stood, lost in wonder, her gaze was drawn to a Thought Ship heading south. Thought Ships were one of the Alleshi's more recent creations. Built of the same translucent fabric as the Castle, they differed from the Holoships found in other parts of Inan, in that they did not require a trained magic user to operate them, and they did not vanish when not in use. Rather they were a halfway point between a purely magical Holo Ship and a conventional aircraft.

"Good morning." The old lady in the market stall smiled at Leah.

"Good morning," said Leah, lowering her gaze from the Thought Ship, by now drifting over the rooftops.

"Raisin bread or sunflower?"

"Sunflower. Please."

"There you go, ducks." The old woman's eyes flicked up, following Leah's gaze. "Those Thought Ships, you never get used to them, do you?"

"No," smiled Leah back at her. "Not if I live to be ninety."

"Me too, ducks. Of course I'll find out sooner than you will."

"I daresay."

"Anything else?"

"What's it like, I wonder?"

"Being ninety? Pain in the arse mostly. Your teeth give out, your knees give in and your bladder gains a mind of its own just as you start to lose yours. Never trust a fart over forty, that's my advice."

Leah looked shocked. "No. Sorry. I meant what it must be like to fly."

A frown slid across the old woman's face.

"Oh! Sorry ducks, sorry." She went back to her stall, arranging her cakes and bread rolls. "I'm sure that's a pain in the arse too. Most things are, I've found."

Leah tucked the sweet roll into her shoulder bag, rustling the greaseproof paper with her books and notepads.

She glanced up at the sky again but the Thought Ship had gone.

Her father had flown in one once. During the last war, her father had –

Her father.

For the second time today his memory had caught her unawares. She shifted the strap on her bag –his bag – and set off towards the Gardens.

As she reached Rendolph's house she slowed her step and tapped on the window. She had known Rendolph since childhood. Despite him being quite the laziest young man in the world, he was as faithful a friend as you could hope for.

An upstairs window opened. It was Rendolph's mother, Glora. "He's not in, lovey," said Glora, shaking the dust from a small rug.

Leah looked up, smiling. "He's gone in early? The age of miracles is still upon us, Glora."

Glora rolled her eyes, despairingly. "The age of miracles has well and truly passed! He never came home last night. Out with Gim again. The two of them are probably asleep in some ditch somewhere. We can only hope a cow covers them in bottom juice and teaches them a lesson."

Reaching work, the guard on sentry duty raised his hand in greeting as Leah made her way towards the Garden gate. The mushrooms rose up like a forest, towering over the high stone wall, their colours gently glowing and pulsating, augmented by the quasi-magical technology the genesmiths had endowed them with in centuries past.

"Good morning guard," called Leah, quickening her pace as she realised the time. "Funny weather today."

"Nothing funny about it Miss. Have you not got the news yet?"

"Another death," said Leah. "Third this month. You'd think we had enough on our plates, wouldn't you?"

"You'd best make your way in quickly, Miss. It wouldn't do for you to hear it from me."

"Hear what?" His eyes lowered, looking away. "Guard,

what's happened? Is it someone here? Has someone in the Garden caught the sickness?"

The guard coughed into his hand, his awkwardness visible.

"Tell me, what's wrong!"

A voice called from inside the gate: "Leah! Leah Carleaf?"

As Leah turned to see to whom the voice belonged, the guard took his chances and retreated to his sentry box, turning up the volume of his earpiece as he did so.

Leah held her palms to the gate, which obligingly swung open, the liquid crystal eyes of the wrought iron Pixies blinking with electronic delight as they recognised a friend.

A man was making his way towards her, his face expressionless, although his eyes were black with worry. He wore an army uniform. Not the dark ochre of the militia, but a light blue, the colour of the Castle guard. A sword hung loosely at his side. An officer, Leah noticed.

"You're late."

Leah blushed, suddenly cross with herself for doing so. "Oh only just. Besides, I was in well after hours three times last week, and anyway I'm owed loads of time in lieu from last month." She paused, wondering why she was explaining herself to a complete stranger. "I'm sorry, do I know you?"

"Captain Rilston, first tier Castle Guard."

"We are honoured, captain. If I'd have realised that my timekeeping was of such importance then I'd have got up extra early."

"If you had then you could would be dead now."

"... dead? Being early is a capital offence these days?"

Rilston's expression stopped Leah's smile in its tracks.

"You had better come with me."

She looked up to see more soldiers in the Garden, their blue uniforms standing out among the seedpods and herbs that grew in the soft womb-like twilight beneath the mushroom's massive spans. Not militia. Castle men again. And then, more remarkable still, she noticed here and there amongst them the bright daisy-yellow armour of Chemical Warriors, military pharmacists under the command of the Sages themselves.

They were searching for something, prodding at bushes with their swords, peering into greenhouses with the faces of men who expect to come under fire at any moment. Twitchy, concentrated, worried.

Leah also realised, with a shudder, that several of the Castle guards were wearing gas masks. One was quite used to seeing old war footage of men in masks, their black armour stained with mud, but it was another thing entirely to see Castle guards dressed for battle. There was something undignified and faintly tragic in seeing them forage in the bushes in their spotless blue ceremonial uniforms; their bright chrome bayonets reflecting back what little light there was in the murk of the Garden. And yet, despite everything, these were men who had sworn to defend the Mage with their own blood. Even so, what could make them grovel in the dirt looking for –?

For what? The thought hit her like a slap in the face.

"What's happened? The news said there had been another death, but why the need for soldiers? Captain, where are all the Gardeners?"

Rilston ran his hand though his hair, pushing his lanky fringe in an unexpectedly boyish way as he brought the scroll of parchment from his satchel.

"Leah Carleaf. Gardener 1st class, apprentice to Chief Gardener Lizall."

"Goodness. Aren't I Miss Popular today?"

"Come with me, please."

Leah fell in behind the captain, following him as he made his way past the searching men to one of the yellow-clad Chemical Warriors. Like the Captain, the Chemical Warrior wore the uniform of an officer, but unlike him, his was without badges of rank.

"I've found her. She was late for work," said Rilston.

The Chemical Warrior looked up at Leah. Like all Chemical Warriors, his pupils were dilated, his eyes red, his gaze distant. He had pale skin.

"Excellent. We feared you were all gone." His voice was slow and sleepy.

"Gone? I don't follow you."

The yellow clad Chemical Warrior drew himself up to his full height and rubbed his eyes. "The sickness came last night. It's taken them all. I'm afraid your colleagues are either dead or dying, Miss Carleaf. We're –" He stretched his arms over his head, like a man waking up from sleep. "We're delighted to find a single Gardener left alive this morning. The only other survivors are the two peasant boys we found, sleeping in the composter."

"No," mumbled Leah, taken aback. "No, this is wrong. The news said that there had been another death, but not this many. Not my friends..."

Rilston coughed. "The news says whatever we tell it to say. I'm sorry, but as of this morning you are the only Gardener left qualified in this part of Allesh."

Something caught Leah's eye, over the Captain's shoulder. It was a body wagon.

"You will have to be tested for the sickness," said the Chemical Warrior, following Leah's gaze. "We believe that it does not spread from person to person, but we are still at a loss to explain how it does infect people. In the meantime we have to expect the worst. Hopefully you are immune."

Leah felt the earth slowly turn beneath her feet. Her friends, her colleagues, all dead. Every one of them. She leaned for support against the trunk of a huge toadstool, older than most of the ramparts of the Castle itself.

The Captain leaned forward, holding her uncertain gaze. "We need you. Your work here is vital. Without the raw materials for the Chemists we are helpless against the storm that's on its way. You do understand, don't you? There will be time to mourn later. Trust me there will be time. But here and now there is work to be done."

Leah sat down, the world suddenly cold and cruel.

"Yes." She said, weakly.

"Good. I'll arrange for help to be sent. My men are needed back at the Castle, but I will order the local militia to assist you in any way you see fit."

The chemist dropped to his knees beside Leah, the hard plastics of his armour clack-clacking in the still, silent air. "You need time. You need help." He slid a bright blue phial into the socket in Leah's wrist. Her eyes met his, and then burned with magical brilliance, before returning to normal once more. She felt suddenly calm. Not drugged or altered, just calm. He pushed a handful into her hands, smiling at her as he did so. "In case you need more," he explained.

"Thank you," she muttered, rising to her feet.

All dead. Yesterday there had been twenty Gardeners here, some her friends, some she didn't know all that well and never would now. Despite the sudden rush of calm keeping her body in check, she knew she was suddenly out of her depth. The fact that Leah was aware she should be panicking at this point, should be crying at the very least, made the calm all the more unreal.

"Oi! Leah!"

She looked up. Rendolph. It was Rendolph!

"Leah! Tell them who we are! They think we're vagrants."

Rendolph and Gim were sat on a bench by the thatched house that served as the office. Two Castle guards stood over them, their rifles held in a casually menacing fashion. The two boys were unshaven, unwashed, unkempt and looked for all the world like they had gone to sleep in a warm compost heap, having fallen down there in a drink fuelled stupor. Which is exactly what had happened.

One of the guards lifted the visor of his gas mask as Leah approached.

"You know these people Miss?"

Leah scowled at them, feeling the delight a parent feels when finding a lost child, followed by the sudden desire to give it the hiding of its life for scaring the wits out of her.

"Never seen them before in my life, soldier. Have them buggered and dropped into the sewers."

"Begging your pardon Miss, but we're not the Navy."

"No, you're right. No point having them make the sewers smell bad is there? Better if you just run them through with your bayonets here and now. Here, pass one over, I'll give you a hand to gut him." Leah turned to Rendolph and Gim. "I thought you were dead, you stupid, lazy, drunken, smelly idiots!"

A toothy smile broke over Rendolph's face. He stood up, his arms wide to embrace her. "Ahh, bless! Come here!"

"Get off!" Leah jumped backwards. "You smell like a –" She was going to say 'a corpse' but thought better of it. "You smell exactly like you. And your brain dead friend."

"She means me," said Gim, proudly, beaming at the

soldiers.

"These two 'men' – and I use the term loosely – are composting assistants, third class, Rendolph and Gim." Leah said.

"Hey! Second class!" said Rendolph.

"No, really, third class. You've just been demoted."

"Who died and put you in charge?" said Gim, laughing and putting his arm round her shoulder. Leah shrugged him off. "What? What did I say?"

She turned to face her friends. "Everyone died. It's just us now. We're all that's left of the Garden staff. It will mean us doing everything. Long hours, no rest, with no thanks and no extra pay."

Rendolph shrugged. "No change there, then."

"No change at all. Gim?"

He looked up, his face far too serious for such an idiot. "Are they really all dead?"

Leah reached out and flicked some straw from his shoulder. "Yes Gim. The sickness took them all. Didn't you think it even a bit strange that the Garden was full of soldiers this morning?" Leah turned to face the soldiers. "These two were working on the new irrigation system. Ever since the well ran dry we've had to take water from further away. I don't know if it's significant to your investigation or not. I merely mention it for the sake of completeness."

Rendolph pulled his shirt off, shaking grass cuttings from his vest.

Leah put her hands on her hips and lifted her gaze to the mushrooms towering above them. It would rain later. There were spores to harvest, sprouts to tend, cuttings to see to. Up through the reaches of the mushrooms and the vines, there was something wrong with the sky. The colour of the sun, the way the windows of the Castle reflected the dim, cold red light. It was all wrong.

Leah realised what it was that was that had been missing from the sunrise all along.

It was hope.

CHAPTER TWO

The attack had come without warning. The Alleshi border patrol, two days out of their barracks, were making good progress in the wastelands that nudged against the Prash-Romaria borders. The patrols had been stepped up in recent weeks, as relationships between the newly created nations in the fragmented former Bethel became ever more frayed. The illness, and the stress it brought with it, had caused many old tensions to re-ignite.

The patrol was cautiously edging its way along the abandoned trench, a relic from the last war, when they found their legs becoming leaden, their limbs heavy. Senses slipped into overdrive as the delicate smell of lavender and spring grasses wafted around them. Instinctively men dropped to their knees, loading rifles with gloved fingers, and trying not to look at the beautiful swirling patterns around them. The sky was now a myriad of colours.

"Take cover! Incendiary!"

The men threw themselves flat on the trench floor, their hands clasped tight across their chests as a sergeant, a veteran of countless skirmishes in the last war, pulled the pin from a grenade and hurled it high into the air. It blossomed briefly, like a rose, like a carnation made of phosphor. The officer at his side gazed up, his eyes seeing what he already knew.

"Genie!" He shouted. "Inject Green now!"

Genies were magical creatures, built by wizards during the war. Used by all sides at one time or another, they were officially outlawed by international agreement. Some still existed here and there, mainly in smaller nations, where resources were lacking for more robust magical defences.

The soldiers pulled green phials from their webbing, and slotted them into their wrist-ports, granting immunity from the Genie's assault. One raw recruit, who had been a farmer's boy but six weeks ago, fumbled through his thick gloves and dropped his. Cursing to himself, he pulled the glove from his hand to better retrieve the phial. The sergeant screamed at him from the other side of the trench. "No! Glove back on! Now!" But it was too late. The soldier stopped and looked up, lost in wonder at the beauty that surrounded him. The pharmaceutical weaponry floating around him entered his bloodstream through the follicles on his unshielded skin. He lifted his bare hand, allowing the gossamer strands to sift through his fingers like warm, scented sand. His eyes filled with tears.

"It's beautiful," he whispered. The Genie swam towards him, its arms reaching out as a lover would reach for his beloved. Oh, but it loved him. Wanted him. How could he not embrace such beauty?

The men in the trench looked away, squeezing their eyes tight shut as the young man fell dead to the ground, hitting the earth like a wet grain sack.

"Rear section, open fire!" yelled the officer, flicking the safety catch from his rifle. Three soldiers jumped up, showering the Genie with a concentrated hail of gunfire, the silver and mistletoe tracer fire ripping through the creature. There was a noise, something between a sigh and the sound of tearing paper, and the Genie melted away to nothingness.

The Sergeant tore off his gas mask, gulping in deep breaths of air. Around him soldiers were doing the same. He knelt by the body of the boy, already pulling his ident tags from his uniform.

"That was the last of our Green, Sergeant." An officer

said. "If we come across another one of these things out here then... Well. Then it'll be a hard fight."

The Sergeant pocketed the tags, reaching to switch off the good luck charms that all recruits wore, despite what the regulations said. No sense in wasting batteries. "Nothing the lads can't handle." They nodded at each other. They both knew this wasn't true.

"Send a message back to the Castle, alerting General Vale. Genie sighted, one casualty. They'll need to alert aircom."

The officer turned his head from side to side, suddenly aware of a stiffness in his shoulders. The result of two weeks on patrol, no doubt. "What's going on, Sergeant? We shouldn't be meeting magical constructs this close to our borders. The Prash-Romarians must be more rattled by the sickness than we thought." He knelt by the dead soldier, his stomach in knots as he mentally began composing the letter to the boy's parents. Worst part of the job; worse than killing someone.

Around him, men peered out into the wilderness, bayonets fixed, safety catches off, the hard plastic armour digging into their mud stained uniforms.

It would be daylight soon.

Perhaps the dawn would bring some hope with it.

The great hall of the Castle was quite rightly considered one of the architectural wonders of the modern world. Even the Alleshi's harshest critics had little choice but to acknowledge it as a work of genius. The pillars that rose from the marble floor twisted and turned as they wove into each other, reaching up into the darkness, defying gravity and simple common sense as they did so.

It should have been impossible for something so delicate to bear even its own weight, and yet somehow they did. The gravity suppression fields that allowed the gossamer strands to hold the vast domed ceiling were maintained by the combination of a powerful repulse engine in the crypts, and the constant prayers of magicians in service to the Mage.

The word 'Castle' never did this place justice, but there was no other word for it. Magic and beauty filled the very sunlight that shone in through the high stained-glass windows. The smooth floors were like an incandescent polished marble that by rights should have been as slippery as ice, and yet held the footing of even the unsteadiest.

Gentle lights flickered a myriad of colours along the walls; the statues seeming half-alive as shadows caressed them. It was common knowledge that one or two of the statues were far more than half-alive. The eyes followed you too closely; their gestures mirrored real life too keenly to be something as simple as mere art.

The two Sages entered from the north transept, their robes hissing softly as they dragged over the cold, smooth floor. The air of magic and chemistry hung thick about them, so that they left a faint trail of condensation on the ground as they passed. Like all Sages, their faces were partially obscured by the hooded robes they wore when outside of the laboratory temples that were their home. Their skin was pale and their clothes damp with the chemicals that protected them.

Following at a respectable distance came four Chemical Warriors, the Sages' honour guard, sworn to protect them at all times. Following strict protocol two warriors always looked outwards, their eyes flitting round the hall as they scoured the shadows, looking for any physical dangers that may lurk there. Another kept his eyes constantly fixed on the Sages, never wavering for a second. His eyes were searching for signs of moral weakness, or signs of possession. The fourth followed behind, his eyes tightly closed. Looking inwards, he focussed on dangers that could not readily be seen by the sane or sober. He focussed on psychological, mental and even spiritual threats.

It would normally take a full five minutes to walk from one side of the hall to the other. The Sages did so today in two, moving with unseemly haste. Even if the Castle itself were on fire, it would not do for them to break into a run, and so their hurried gait was all the more unusual.

The Sages stopped by the door at the south transept. Two blue uniformed Castle guards barred their way, spears crossed threateningly. The Chemical Warriors narrowed their eyes suspiciously; their thumbs rubbing the stoppers on the phials of potion they wore on their uniforms.

"Who comes, in the name of the most high Mage?" shouted one of the guards; his eyes fixed on the middle distance. Respectfully, he avoided eye contact with the Sages.

"Friends," whispered one of the Sages. He made a subtle gesture with his hand. A complicated pheromone spray drifted from his fingertips, the particles carrying complex biological data through the air. The LED jewels on the guards' spear glowed a soft azure as the bio-data was analysed and deemed acceptable by the tiny artificial mind lodged there.

"Advance friends!"

Passing through the door, and out of earshot, the Sages at last lowered their hoods. The taller of the two turned to face his companion, his features white with rage.

"What is this madness, Niaal? Are things so mismanaged

that protocol has been abandoned, all manners allowed to die?" His friend, shorter and stockier smiled calmly back at him.

Whereas Grefno was tall and nervous in demeanour, Niaal was shorter, with a gentle benign air. He radiated calm and reassurance, the very picture of the aloof magic user that the Sages of Allesh prided themselves to be. He had distinguished himself in the war, and had quickly risen through the ranks of the military wizards to become a Sage in the Castle. He had been one of the officers responsible for bringing about peace in Western Bethel, and indeed was among those who had rallied around the Mage when he put himself forward as their leader.

"Peace, Grefno."

"Peace? Niaal, we are nearly in a state of war again!"

"We have been at war before. We survived, and we rose above it. The treaty, signed by all the Mages of all the lands of Inan saw to that, and granted us peace. We have all seen the horror of war first hand, and yet we still live."

"For which I am grateful." Grefno followed him along the vast corridor; his face wrought with worry. "There have been... reports, though."

Niaal smiled "Reports? There are always reports, I am sure they are nothing."

Grefno drew a circle in the air, producing an image of a group of soldiers, black-armoured frontline troops. "See this? Only this morning one of our patrols was attacked by a Genie, of all things! And close to our borders, too. This should not be tolerated. We should be at work, we should be finding a cure for this illness, not spending our time seeing our patrols attacked by the magical constructs of foreign powers! Wretched things were outlawed by the peace treaty. The Prash-Romarians should know better than allow their continued use."

The corridor opened into a large wood panelled octagonal room, adorned with paintings of the Sages and heroes of the Great War. Waiting in the middle of the room stood an officer in the brown of the local militia, although in affectation of a cavalry style. As the Sages approached, he squared his shoulders and bowed his head in greeting.

"Honoured Sages, you sent for me." The Sages' entourage of Chemical Warriors surrounded him, probing with their eyes, reading his heartbeat, the electricity on his skin, the movement of his pupils. "I realise how unusual this must be for you," the officer continued nervously, trying to ignore the Chemical Warriors, "but please be assured it is a very real pleasure for me. One so rarely gets the chance of an audience with such learned company."

Niaal smiled back, a superior expression on his face. He nodded at the Warriors and they glided back, standing at equal intervals around the edges of the room. "The pleasure is all ours, Captain Krillan. We are but simple men of science. Cloistered here in the Castle we owe our continued safety to the bravery of men such as yourself." Krillan bowed his head once more, unsettled but deeply flattered to be so acknowledged.

Grefno frowned. "And The Mage, of course." he muttered.

Niaal looked up him, a pleased look on his round face. "But of course. Preserve him."

Niaal sat down in one of the many high backed wooden chairs that were set into the wall of the room, but Grefno kept pacing around the captain, full of nervous energy.

"Tell me Captain... Krillan, was it? How is containment of the sickness progressing? Have you been able to limit the spread?"

Krillan shuffled his feet, his hands twitching restlessly by his side. He smiled weakly. "Honoured Sages, I am doing my best in exceptional circumstances with appallingly limited resources. I asked for a squad of regular infantry, and yet have to make do with..." He paused. "With militia men." He said the word as if his mouth were full of vinegar. "I am doing the best I can. They need to be driven constantly; they require a firm hand to keep them in place. I am pushing them to their utmost, naturally."

Niaal sighed. "Naturally." He stood up, adjusting his robes, flicking at an imaginary fleck of dust. "But have you actually contained the spread of the sickness? Have you done what you were asked?"

Grefno placed a soft hand on his colleague's shoulder. "I'm sure the Captain is doing his best, dear friend."

"I'm sure he is, and yet the facts remain, Grefno. The sickness must be contained. We are no closer to understanding what causes it than we were this time last month." Niaal gestured with his hand, casting a minor spell. At once, a window appeared in the air. Straining his eyes Krillan could see it showed a view of the hospital, the sick and dying lined up in beds. In another corner it showed a map of the immediate lands around the castle, with points in red where the sickness had been reported. A complex pattern of brightly coloured spheres and lines appeared to one side, representing what Krillan assumed to be possible cures. There were many more things that he did not recognise, and knew he could never hope to.

Niaal pointed a long pale finger at the window. "We should divert less energy into understanding it and more into containing it. The Captain here will see to that. I take it the village has been cordoned off?"

Krillan looked up, eager to bring good news "It has.

Although the inhabitants are as yet unaware of it. They will find out soon enough, of course. Tomorrow is market day. When they see the empty stalls, they'll work it out for themselves."

Grefno made his way to the magic window, gazing with interest at the jewel bright pixels that hung in the air. "This is the third outbreak this week."

Niaal nodded. "If the disease is airborne, and we must hope that it is not, it could breach the Castle defences. It needs to be contained at all costs."

Grefno rubbed his eyes. "Nearly all costs. We will not have this place sterilised." Krillan startled at the words. He knew what sterilisation entailed. He felt a thrill of terror at the word. Sterilisation was a military term for the complete and total destruction of life in an area, even down to microbe level. As a form of warfare it was now banned, but the remote possibility of future use remained, as a last ditch solution to containment of disease.

Grefno turned slowly, facing him. " I take it you have been screened and are safe?"

Krillan burst into an instant sweat, his hands clammy by his sides. "I have followed all decontamination protocols to the letter, honoured Sage!"

"But the protocols don't work! If they did we wouldn't be in this mess, would we?"

"But honoured Sage, if they don't work then why do we still adhere to them?"

Niaal turned away from the window, smiling kindly at the uncomfortable soldier. "It helps maintain public confidence. Gives them something to do while dying. However, I asked the Captain to join us here, and personally oversaw his screening. He's as clean as snow. For the moment." Niall turned to face Krillan. "We need to keep the villagers alive," he said. "Without them there will be no one to tend the Gardens, and without the Gardens we cannot effectively defend our borders. What level clearance have you been given, Captain?"

"Level three."

Niaal blinked twice, triggering a file upload. "I have just given you level four."

Krillan bowed, his heart pounding with excitement. "I am honoured."

"We know," said Niaal.

"Thank you for your confidence in me. As a professional soldier I am too young to have had the privilege of serving my country in war, obviously, but all the same I hope I would not be found wanting if tested."

Niaal sighed. "We are at war against an illness, Captain. We are not fighting an enemy we can readily understand. If it were a simple case of sending men over the top, of throwing numbers at it, then we would."

Krillan squared his shoulders. "And I should volunteer to be the first."

"I'll make sure we bear you in mind, Captain." Grefno said, turning from the window.

Niaal drew a shape in the air. It showed the ambushed patrol the two Sages had discussed earlier, the images transmitted from suit cameras. The men were pointing and firing at indistinct shapes in the air, whispers of coloured smoke, lit by magical brilliance from within. Niaal continued. "Our neighbours remain a real and constant threat. These images show a border patrol, ambushed yesterday by magical attack."

"Then surely this is a threat for the army to deal with? This is our area of expertise." Krillan said. "Unless..." and here he paused. "Unless you think the illness itself comes from our neighbours?"

"I think we have said enough for now, Krillan. Rest

assured all is being done." Grefno made a gesture and the window vanished. "You will return to the village and enforce the cordon around it. It may be that we require you to stay there until a cure is found."

"Honoured Sages, and if a cure is not found?" The silence hung heavy in the room.

Grefno smiled sadly at him. "Then you will no doubt do your duty. You may go, Captain."

Krillan stood to attention, clicked his heels, and with a smart about turn marched cleanly out of the door and to his duty.

At first it had been just a whisper, barely that. An almost imperceptible voice in the night speaking to him of power and re-birth. As the creature grew that whisper had increased in volume until the voice of the thing had become almost deafening. Now it writhed in its lair and sung and wailed of a power unimaginable. A power that would chain the greatest Mages of Inan to his will. A power that would flow through him and encompass the entire planet.

Niaal looked at the shell of a man that sat on the throne before him. Already his flesh was beginning to atrophy as the creature took hold, spreading its taint through the channels of magic that flowed through the Mage. Niaal took a step back as the Mage's belly began to distend, a vile liquid beginning to trickle from his pores. The transformation was alarmingly rapid and Niaal began to worry that the creature would bear its hideous progeny before his plans had a chance to come to fruition. No matter, with the whole of Allesh ignorant to his scheme and General Vale playing into his hands, he still had control. If the end of the old order was to come sooner than Niaal had at first anticipated, well, that suited him just fine.

"Goodnight Pillian," he said, leaning over and closing the Mage's eyes.

Niaal surveyed the throne room. What had once been the seat of all power in Allesh was now beginning to crumble as the Mage's last powers diminished. Soon the whole Castle would succumb and once its last remains had sunk into the soil, Niaal would construct a new demesne where the whole of Inan would come to pay tribute. And that palace would never crumble and Niaal's power would never wane.

Leaving the throne room through a concealed door he descended into the darkness, weaving his way through the tunnels beneath the Castle and towards the lair of the worm.

Leah threw down her pen and sat back in her chair, rubbing her eyes. She picked up the clock beside her and let out a moan. Midnight. For the fifth night in succession she had been at her desk until midnight, studying for exams that she might now never even take. She had read the same paragraph three times in a row, and knew this was her brain telling her to stop.

She went over to the bedroom window and flung it open, enjoying the sudden sharp of the cold night air.

Tip-toeing out onto the landing, she gently eased open the door to her mother's bedroom. As usual, Saran was lying on her side, an arm outstretched towards the empty space beside her. Leah silently closed the door and went back to her room. An owl hooted outside.

Looking along the road she saw the night watchman making his slow steady way, the lamp hanging from the pike slung over his shoulder. All seemed calm and all was in its place.

Leah shivered, and pulled the window closed, drawing the curtains. She slid into bed and blew a kiss to the candle on the other side of the room. It interpreted the gesture and blinked the room into gentle darkness.

Leah was up early, leaving her mother a note saying a), that she loved her, b) sorry about leaving the kitchen in a mess and c), that she loved her again. Being the first at work was a novelty she thought she'd never see, but the sudden emergency meant that everything had changed. Despite the fear and panic that had gripped the village, Leah felt excited.

It was just a sickness, therefore it could be cured. That's why they tended the Gardens. They made ingredients for the Sages to use in their magic, and medicines for treating the sick.

As she was now the most senior person on site, Leah found herself rising to the task in a way she would not have thought possible only a week ago. She felt guilty every time it crossed her mind, but she realised that this was what she had always wanted. Managing the Garden, ordering the production of herbs and potions, running the whole show.

Today she was synthesising chemicals from one of the larger fungi. Fifty feet up, she worked at a computer terminal set in a small ledge, carved into the side of the great mushroom.

Heights didn't bother Leah. Falling and dying bothered

her. Falling and being badly injured and then dying in unending agony stretched out over months and years worried her more. But not the actual heights themselves. Best thing was to keep your mind on the job at hand.

"No use. Bored." She switched off the terminal, tapped her harness once, and jumped off the ledge. The zip line sung and whined as she gently slid down to earth. As the ground rushed up to greet her she saw Gim and Rendolph making their way through the gates, smiling like idiots. Which was only appropriate, when all was said and done.

"Good morning gentlemen. I use the term sarcastically, of course." She brushed past them, pulling a clipboard from her satchel as she passed by.

"Sorry we're late," said Gim, helpfully. Rendolph slapped him on the back of his head.

"We're not late. We're early."

"Oh yeah. Sorry we're early. Weren't our fault."

Leah laughed. "Did you get the rest of those seed pods sent off last night like I asked? Or will I have to take my top off and wrestle you in warm scented mud as a punishment?"

The two boys looked at each other, suddenly very unsure on what the correct answer was at this point in time. "Um..." began Gim, his jaw slacker than usual.

"Too late!" said Leah, snapping her clipboard shut. "I want the fertiliser servers up and running within the hour. I'm sure that will be much more fun than seeing my lithe, toned, yet delightfully feminine naked body."

Making their way into the staff room, Gim and Rendolph hung up their coats and quickly changed into their work overalls. Neither of them commented on the rows of unused overalls hanging on the pegs. Or why they were unused. Only last week there had been thirty

Gardeners here. Now there were just the three of them. The lockers and shelves were still full of personal effects, pictures of loved ones, spare tools and books. The clutter of their dead colleagues was almost unbearable.

Gim knocked over a walking stick. It had belonged to Fricka, the aborealist. "We should tidy this place up," he said. "Someone should come and get their things. It's not right having them here like this. It's depressing."

Rendolph picked up Fricka's stick and put it back in its place. "It'll be alright. Don't worry."

Gim glared back at him, eyes suddenly full of tears "How? How will it be alright? They're all dead, Rendolph. They're all dead and we don't know what killed them or if we'll be next."

Leah didn't know what to say. He was right, this was terrible. Awful. She put her hand in her bag and pulled out one of the small blue phials the Chemical Warrior had given her. "Here," she said, handing it to Gim. "Take this. It'll help calm you down."

Gim took it, glaring at it defiantly. "Bloody chemicals. They control us too much. We should be in tears, should be grief stricken!" He looked up. "We should be too afraid to work here."

Rendolph put a hand on his shoulder. "I know. There'll be time for that later. Really, there will, but right now we need to get the job done."

Glaring at his friend, Gim slid the blue phial into his wrist-port, furious at the wave of calm and well being that shot through him. Rendolph smiled, then gestured at the overalls that hung accusingly on the wall. "It's what they would have wanted."

Out of respect for her friend Leah counted to twenty, allowing the Blue time to kick in before speaking up. "No it isn't," she coughed. "What they would have wanted was to still be alive so they could make your life miserable for being idle useless half-wits."

"That's not funny," Gim said, starting to smirk.

"No," said Leah. "It isn't. So why are you laughing?"

"Because the Blue is making me feel happy when I know I should be miserable. It's just not right. Bloody scientists, can't get anything right, can they?"

Leah picked up her workbag and slung it over her shoulder. "Come on," she said. "Let's get on with it. We need to harvest the spores before lunchtime, or we'll never get the extract up to the Castle in time. Dammit, where are those soldiers we were promised?"

"Ah." Rendolph looked guilty. "I passed them on the way in. They're by the main gate awaiting orders. Forgot to mention them. Sorry."

Leah playfully smacked him around the head with her bag.

As Leah stood in the soft morning rain, she felt a sudden deep connection to it all. To history, to her people. This was what she was here for. This was what they worked so hard for. To preserve their way of life. To defend their borders against the enemy, and maintain the health of the citizens within.

The Castle shimmered in the distance. Somewhere within its walls, the Mage sat. Leah turned her gaze to the village. There were thirty new households grieving, children who would grow without a parent. Did the Mage know their pain; did he share in it? Or was he above even that?

Thirty Gardeners, struck down by the sickness. There had been many theories doing the rounds, as to why it picked on some people and not others.

Something had happened here, in the Garden, while the three of them had been absent. But what? The official explanation was that one of the herbsmen must have brought the sickness in with him and infected the others. But surely the incubation time couldn't be so immediate? It would take days for someone to get sick. If indeed it was a sickness. The Chemical Warriors had suspected that it might be some new biological weapon, and yet there was no trace.

What then? Why these people here, why now? There had been isolated cases in the village for the last two months. Unrelated people suddenly taking sick and dying. From first symptom to death was ten days. There was no cure.

No. That wasn't right. There is always a cure. She remembered her father's words. There is always a cure, but first you have to find it.

They would find a cure. The Mage would find a cure.

The soldiers were waiting for her at the gate. One or two made a half-hearted effort to come to attention, but thought better of it. She was not an officer. She was a Gardener. A burly Sergeant tipped his hat and smiled.

"Morning, Miss. Three Company militia reporting for duty." Leah smiled at him. It was Wallas, an old friend of the family. Like Leah's father, Wallas had been a veteran of the Great War.

"Good morning, Sergeant Wallas. Thank you for coming at such short notice. With the Gardeners all gone we have no alternative but to call in help from the military. You are most welcome."

"It's alright, Miss. Wish it were in happier circumstances is all. Where do you want us to start?" Wallas was the same age as her mother, and it took Leah by surprise that he was looking to her to lead.

"That's a good question. I don't know really. I'm not a manager, not used to this sort of thing at all."

"Well, imagine we're new starters, first day on the job."

Leah smiled, gratefully. "Good idea. I'll take you to the changing rooms, get you kitted out, show you the toilets, kitchen, that sort of thing. Then I'll see about getting some sort of plan together. It'll take a while to show you how to tend the plants properly, but there's no reason why we shouldn't get back on track with tilling and sowing."

Wallas shouldered his rifle, casually. "Very good Miss. Lead on."

Leah turned to face the soldiers, waiting expectantly. "Right, if you'd all like to follow me then –"

"Squad! Attention. By the right, MARCH!" Wallas bellowed.

"Ow! That was right in my ear."

"Sorry, Miss."

"It's alright. Come on, let's see if we can't sort this mess out together, before your beloved captain gets involved, eh?"

"Captain Krillan is a stickler for detail, Miss."

"Yes. Yes he certainly is. If by that you mean he's a prick."

"Oh, not for me to say, Miss. That he's a prick and everyone knows it. Wouldn't do, would it?" Wallas smiled at her. "He was a good old boy, your dad. He'd have been proud to see you like this. Running things. Sorting things out. His job meant so much to him. He said plants could cure anything if you only found the right one."

"Thank you Sergeant. He spoke very highly of you too."

CHAPTER THREE

The woods were a mile or so outside the village and, whilst not part of the Gardens as such, they had long been assumed to be more or less the preserve of those who worked there. In the summer months the villagers would often stroll through the woods. Children would play in the branches and young men would hunt rabbits or wildfowl. Some people came here to gather firewood, flowers or forage for edible fungus and wild fruits. It was a good place, and one that belonged to everyone, young and old. Leah loved the woods more than the Garden, truth be told. She delighted in the wildness and unpredictability of nature. It was also a good place for a Gardener to gather specimens from time to time.

Despite the increased workload of running the Garden, Leah thoughts increasingly began turning back to her approaching exams, and she found herself wondering if the plants there might be of some use in her studies. If she could produce a new magical application for an everyday species, then it would help her grades no end.

As she made her way along the road that lead towards the woods, she could see soldiers ahead, unloading something from the back of a transport. Krillan's men, not the boys helping Wallas in the Garden. They were unravelling razor wire and sandbags. A yellow barrier had been erected across the road.

"What's all this about?" Leah asked the nearest guard.

"Roadblock, Miss. Orders from the Castle."

"Alright. I won't be long. I'm just off to the woods. Make sure you remember to let me back in again, won't you?"

"Sorry Miss, no one's to leave once the roadblock's in

place."

"Yes, but it's not in place, is it? And you've obviously seen me, so you'll remember to let me back in again." The guard stared at her blankly. "Oh this is getting us nowhere, is there an officer here? A sergeant or something?"

A voice sprung up from behind the transport. "Ah. Miss Carleaf. A pleasure as always." Krillan's voice.

"Captain Krillan, I need to go to the woods. There are valuable specimens there that I'm due to harvest today."

"Miss Carleaf, we are in the middle of a national emergency. The Castle, village and the surrounding area are to be cordoned off. Anyone attempting to cross the border will be shot. Dreadful inconvenience this I know, but there we are. Orders are orders."

"Captain, this sickness, whatever it is, may well be airborne you know. Putting up a roadblock isn't going to stop it."

"Thank you, Miss Carleaf. Obviously that had never occurred to us." The smile never left Krillan's face. "However, if a person was carrying the disease and wanted to cross the border then a roadblock and a rifleman could at least contain them."

"What? So we all die here?"

Krillan coughed, awkwardly. "Yes Miss Carleaf. If need be, then we die here. We have our orders, and will honour them."

"Look Captain, I'm sorry, I didn't mean to be rude. Please forgive me. However, I really do have to get across to those woods over there." She pointed to a copse, about half a mile distant. "There's no one living there, at least there shouldn't be, and I promise to come straight back. Feel free to keep a marksman on me at all times in case I do a runner."

"Yes, well, sorry to keep you Miss Carleaf, but I have

a lot to do. Sorry for the inconvenience this causes, but there we are. Orders." He turned on his heel and marched off, barking out instructions to a group of soldiers who were making a mess of erecting a barrier.

Leah looked at the wood and sighed. So close, and yet it might as well be a million miles off for all the difference it made.

She looked up as a Thought Ship make its way towards the Castle. "Alright for you lot in there. Don't see anyone putting roadblocks up to stop aircraft."

With a humph, loud enough for the soldiers to notice, Leah made her way back to the village with the empty basket slung over her shoulder.

Mornings were always worst on the anniversary. The worst day of the year, without doubt, but one which thankfully had become less painful with the passage of time.

The first anniversary had been awful. Worse than she had expected. The second was no better, and the third no real improvement on that. But she had flu on the fourth, and somehow the fever and the headache seemed more real to her than the pain of loss. She realised then, with a rush of guilt, that she was getting over it. At that point she decided it was time to let herself heal. Besides, she had Leah to care for. The child was marvellous, but she was too young to carry her mother like this.

Saran was not a strong person, but she could be very stubborn. If she coped at all it would be because she had decided to and there was no one who could tell her otherwise.

Leah was so like her father that, at times, it was too

much for Saran to even look at her. But, day by day, she had forced herself to see this as a good thing. He was gone, but he lived on. His daughter carried his name, his good looks, and above all else, his love for his work.

They had been inseparable.

Until the night of his death.

Saran moved from room to room, tidying the house, picking up Leah's books, and getting the table ready for supper. It was while she was washing her hands that she noticed the bluish tint to her skin. At first she thought it food dye, and tried rubbing it off with stronger soap, but it would not budge. Moving into the light of the living room, she rolled her sleeve up to see that the rash – if rash it was – had spread up her entire left arm. She furrowed her brow, trying to remember what she had had to eat recently. She was not allergic to anything that she knew of, but it was not unheard of to suddenly develop an unfortunate reaction to something, she supposed.

No. Nothing out of the ordinary. She decided the best thing to do was to not worry about it and see if it was still there in the morning. The apothecary could always take a look tomorrow. Probably be gone before morning.

Saran put away the last of the dishes, brushed some crumbs from her sleeve, and fell to floor.

He pulse raced, her body temperature went through the roof, as she lay on the kitchen floor convulsing. She had struck her head on a corner of the table as she went down, and a small trickle of blood ran from a cut just behind her ear. As she fell into unconsciousness all Saran could see was the face of her dead husband.

And with that, everything went black.

Leah was supervising the new recruits, walking them through seed dressing when the comm terminal bleeped, alerting her to an incoming message. It was Rendolph's mother, Glora.

"Leah, it's your mother. She's been taken ill. I don't know what's the matter with her. I've sent for the doctor but I think you need to come home, love."

Leah jogged from the seeding beds back to the office, pulling off her overalls as she ran. Over the past three days the Gardens had returned to something like normality, and she had been delighted at the ease with which the militia had adapted to their new role. They still had a long way to go and a lot to learn, but, at this rate, full production would be back before they knew it.

Leaving the Garden she spotted Captain Krillan and his entourage making its way towards her. "Oh perfect. Great timing." She muttered to herself. Ducking to avoid them behind a water tank, she turned the corner out of sight and broke into a run. She didn't stop until she got to her front door.

Glora was there to meet her. "She's upstairs. Don't know what's wrong with her, she was like it when we found her."

Leah nodded and went in, dropping her bag on an armchair, and ducking as she passed the low beams that led to the narrow staircase. She could hear voices from the top rooms. Two stairs at a time she bounded to Saran's room, to see her mother in bed, her skin pale.

It was the sickness. It was here.

She looked up, horrified, to see the two men in the room attending to her mother. They both wore facemasks. She recognised one as Kefan, the village doctor. They looked in panic and alarm as she tried to enter the room, before slamming the door in her face.

"Leah, stay outside! Your mother has the sickness!"

"Let me in right this instant or I promise you I will kick the door down." She looked at the sturdy oak door; the huge wrought iron hinges and steel bolt, built to last. "Let me in this instant or I will go outside and find a huge muscled man and get him to kick this door down for me!"

"Leah   –"

"I mean it, open the door!"

"Leah, it's me, Doctor Barrot. Go down to the kitchen table and you'll find my bag. There's another mask there. Put it on and then open the blue box and take the grey phial inside. It's a standard anti-body and should fight off any residual germs that might be lurking in the air. Your mother has the sickness. We don't know how ill she is yet, but you catching it won't help her one bit! Now go downstairs, do as I ask and then you can come in."

Leah closed her eyes and bumped the door gently with her head, and then went downstairs and did as she was told.

The grey phial hurt like hell. She felt it rush through her body like a pack of hunting dogs after their quarry. She felt sick, her head hurt and there was a ringing in her ears. She looked at the phial and read through the list of possible side effects, before dropping the empty container in the bin and making her way back upstairs.

Militia men arrived, waddling through the streets in bacteriological warfare suits none of them had worn since basic training, and which no longer fitted as well as they once might have. Soon the whole street was cordoned off as Chemical Warriors went from house to house, taking blood samples and saliva swabs. Thankfully no one else seemed to have the sickness. A military vehicle arrived, and Saran was taken away in a translucent oxygen tent to the hospital, a wing of which had been given over solely to the sickness and its victims.

Word spread very quickly in the village, and soon people were calling their children inside and leaving pets out in the yard. It was as if there was something heavy sitting on the very spirit of the village itself. Like something wrapped around it, squeezing the life from it.

Leah sat in her mother's chair at the table. She held a blue phial in her hand, rolling it from finger to finger. She thought of her father. And she thought also of his sense of duty, of his passion for getting the job done. Of what it meant to face down disaster. She took a deep breath and slid the phial into her wrist.

Saran was not the first patient admitted that day, nor was she the last. One by one the sick started to arrive. No one expected any of them to make it through the night and, indeed, one or two of the more elderly patients didn't live to see sunrise. But the vast majority, although in a serious condition, were still holding onto life come morning. And against all the odds, the majority were still there by midday. Whatever was wrong with them, it wasn't the same sickness that had killed the workers in the Garden. Or at least it wasn't as severe for some reason. The doctors weren't sure if this was a good thing or a bad thing. In one sense it would be better if the disease remained a constant, something they could measure with some accuracy; then they would have a better chance of finding a cure if such a thing existed.

But as things stood at the moment the sickness was completely unpredictable in how it effected a patient and what symptoms it displayed.

The Barrots ran the small local hospital. Kefan and Kadia were husband and wife. They had moved to the village some years previously, and had quickly endeared themselves to the locals. They were as well known for their skills as physicians as they were for their legendary fertility, having some twelve children between them. Leah had known them since she was a little girl, and had always felt at ease with them. They had been there when her father died, and had seen her through all of the ups and downs of everyday life.

They had helped Saran deal with the constant aching sadness that at times threatened to destroy her, not through medicine alone, although that had its part, but by simply listening, and by helping her to mend herself by engaging with normality.

Leah sat in the wood beamed hall that served as the waiting room. It had previously been the canteen, but there were so many recent admissions that every spare room had been taken up. Non-critical patients had been sent home, freeing up bed space.

"Leah?" It was Kadia, scrubbing her hands with a wipe. "How are you doing?" Kadia was the complete opposite of Kefan. Where he was short and rotund, she was tall and willowy, with long grey hair. Leah had always thought her quite beautiful, and could never equate the elegance she constantly showed with the nature of her work, dealing with sickness and disease in all its gory detail.

"I don't know. I don't know how I am. I think a lot of that depends on how my mother is. How bad has she got it? She looked awful."

"You've seen her then?"

"Only through plastic sheeting. They wouldn't let me touch her. Is she going

to get better?"

Kadia sat down on the pine bench next to her, her hands folded, silent. Outside, a transport was pulling into the drive in front of the hospital. More sick people waiting to be helped, no doubt.

"Your mother has a particularly bad chest infection. We are treating it as best we can, but are short of supplies." She looked at Leah squarely and openly, her face calm and serious. "People have died, Leah, you need to accept that. The elderly and sick seem particularly vulnerable, but your mother is fit and strong. There is every hope for her."

"The Gardeners, they weren't old. Most of them were my age."

Kadia reached out a hand and felt Leah's wrist, checking her pulse, but also casting a critical eye at her wrist-port. "How much Blue have you been taking?"

Leah took a deep breath, paused and let it out. "Loads. I was going to lie just then. I was going to say 'a little bit now and then', but these last few days, since, you know, since everyone died...? Well, frankly I've been shovelling the stuff in. One of the Chemical Warriors gave a load to me. Probably to make sure that the Gardens remained operational. The side effects are driving me mad, though. I keep making constant inappropriate comments. Cracking jokes about everything all the time. I don't think it's particularly funny. I don't think I'm funny... which might be one reason why no one seems to be laughing. I do think that gallows humour is a coping mechanism of sorts, albeit a fairly unpleasant one, it's just that I wish I could find a different way to cope. I'm considering an alternative therapy and might try losing myself in deep erotic abandonment with a squad of muscular, tanned firemen." Kadia raised a quizzical eyebrow "No really, I am. Properly rude sexual experimentation. Tag-team intercourse, no holds barred physical gratification with no thought to the consequences." She paused, suddenly red faced. " Or perhaps a nice picnic?"

Kadia finished looking at her wrist and smiled. "I'd go for the picnic if I were you. A lot of the local lads are quite uncouth and probably keep their shoes on while doing the naughty stuff. Firemen's boots are flame retardant and go all the way up to their knees. Just think of the chafing."

"Thanks. You're not going to ask me to stop are you?"

"Stop what? Destroying your social life with mind altering chemicals, or stop you cheering up vast armies of civic servants?"

"Either really."

"You need to ease off the Blue, if you can. It stops you feeling emotional pain. Your mother is ill. You should be feeling things, frankly, no matter how inconvenient it might be for your work. As for the other business, they're your rude bits and it's not for me to say. But again, just think of the chafing."

"Thanks."

"It's going to be all right, you know? I know it seems impossible right now, but things have a way of working out. It just seems impossible when you're as young as you are, but I do understand, truly I do. I was young once." She laughed, warmly. "Kefan wasn't, of course. He was born his current age. Which might explain why he never really bonded with his own mother."

"Current age or current size?

"Both, really."

"Ouch. Chafing again?"

"Hmm. Just a bit."

Leah stood up, straightening her work dress as she did so. "When can I see her?"

"Not today. We've got her in isolation. If we can contain the disease, then that will be a small victory in itself." Kadia put a gentle hand on Leah's shoulder. "Go home and get some rest. Science explains the world, discovers it. But science won't be enough. It's going to take magic to solve our problems, and for that we need the Sages to do their work. And for that we need people like you alive and well."

"Right. So it all hangs on me then? No pressure."

"Eat sensibly, avoid strong drink, talk about your feelings and get lots of sleep."

"I'll see you in the morning."

"I'll let you know if there are any developments." Kadia held out her hand. Leah shook it, feeling the weathered dry skin against the softness of her own palm.

"And Leah?"

"Yes?"

"Don't go talking to any strange firemen on the way home."

The sun was setting over the woods as Leah made her way from the hospital down to the part of the village where she lived. The inns were open, light spilling out invitingly from within, but they sounded subdued, half-empty. It made sense. People were at home, scared to go out in case the sickness somehow was passed on to them. In case they brought it home to their loved ones. Leah paused to look at the Castle, towering high in the distance. The light caught its walls and towers and shone and sparkled with a bright orange glow in the early evening. She hoped to whatever Gods there were that her mother would be alive in the morning.

Anything was treatable. Anything.

She looked towards the Gardens. The giant mushrooms were glowing softly in the fading light. She hoped the night shift were watering the seedlings properly. Too much water and... she sighed.

"Let it go, girl. Go to bed."

Grefno rubbed his eyes and viewed the image once again. He had been sitting here for four hours now and still it made no sense. Patterns, projections, probabilities, all swam in front of him like tadpoles composed of data. It made no sense. Every charm, every strategy, had failed him. He was entirely unsure whether the sickness could be conquered before it claimed the lives of everyone in Allesh.

The last rays of the sunset through the vast lead light windows caught the dust particles hanging in the air; making golden patterns like bubbles in a glass of cold beer. Every now and then a tiny robot the size of a grain of sand joined the pattern, adding flecks of silver and green to the swirling gold. The air in the Castle was thick with them. Grefno leaned back into the polished wood of his chair. The size of a throne in a less civilised land, the chair held his shape perfectly. Fine monofilament wires like gossamer, like spiders' webs in the first mists of morning, wove their way out from the dark grained wood, feeding him with ideas and magic.

Nothing made sense about this. The sickness, on the face of it, was straightforward enough. And yet when probed, it defied explanation at every turn. Every protein chain, every strand of living matter seemed to twist and turn out of his understanding, out of his grasp.

At first he had discounted the idea that the sickness might somehow be magical in nature, but now he was not so sure. There were things about it that certainly seemed to be magical in origin, but then so much was, that it could just be background noise.

There was certainly nothing mechanical about it. No robots the size of blood cells replicating. Likewise there were none of the other obvious dangers one might expect. No golems made from living matter at the molecular level rampaging through immune systems.

And yet what else could it be?

Gently extricating himself from the lattice that held him in the chair, he made his way to the window that looked out to the West. You could see a long way from here, but today his eyes didn't strain to the horizon, and instead went to the nearby village, sheltering in the snug of the valley below the Castle wall. There were towns and cities across the land, but the village had a special place in the life of the Castle. The people living there were the cleaners, the cooks, the guards, but also a permanently visible symbol of what the Castle stood for.

There was a view, not one that Grefno adhered to, that the Mage kept the villagers close to anchor him to normality. To remind him of what he was here to protect, and of what he had once been in the days before he had become a Mage.

Beyond the village, Grefno let his eyes gaze on the Gardens. The massive plants rose above the walls, not as high as the walls of the Castle, but almost as imposing in their own quiet way. The magnificent trees swayed, silhouetted by the setting sun, whilst pulsating lights shimmered across the vast mushrooms.

As a Sage, Grefno could see things hidden from ordinary eyes. He looked at the Garden with more than mere vision, with magical insight, with a philosophical understanding. He could see the strands that bound the two together. The emotional bonds between the people and their Mage, and the framework of enchantments that hung in the air above them. Magical defences that no spell or smart bomb could ever hope to penetrate. In theory, the Garden should have been the safest place in the land, apart from the Castle itself.

So why were most of the Gardeners now lying cold in the autopsy rooms in the bowels of the Castle? It made no sense. The plants themselves, although not exactly safe, were at least in the hands of trained people. Men and women who knew their craft well enough not to be poisoned through negligence.

Niaal, his equal in every way, had postulated that there may have been some breakdown in the processing of the chemicals. A manufacturing error that had resulted in a deadly toxin being released into the air, but again this made no sense. Why were there no traces of it in the leaves and grass inside the Garden? Why were there no traces in the clothes of the victims? Likewise, something as straightforward as food poisoning seemed out of the question, given that none of them ate there as a point of order, given the complicated chemical make up of many of the plants.

Grefno heard the door slide open on its wooden runners, and turned to see Niaal standing behind him.

"The results of the latest autopsies are in, Grefno. I thought you should be the first to know."

"Well? Do they tell us anything?"

"Only that one or two liked a drink, one was addicted to Green, and one had a sexually transmitted disease that he wasn't telling anyone about. Nothing out of the ordinary. Fairly standard for a sample this size."

"Does it tell us why they died?"

Niaal drew a shape in the air and a pictogram blinked into existence, sparkles of glitter falling through the air as it rejoiced itself into being. "All the same and yet all different. For some reason, which we can't establish, their bodies were all responding as if they had lost a major organ: heart, lungs, liver, things you can't do without. One body was trying to compensate for a failing kidney that was actually fine. Another brain was being told that the liver was no longer working. It seems that the sickness blocks information being sent to the brain so that it thinks that whole areas of the body have shut down. The brain tries to compensate for the perceived loss and that is what actually kills the person. We've tried interfering with the signal, heading it off before it gets to any part of the brain that makes decisions about basic body functions, but with no luck. In real terms, they are otherwise healthy people. There is nothing wrong with any of them."

Grefno sighed.

"But what's causing it? The chances of them all just deciding to up and die on us like this with no real obvious cause. It's... well, it's ridiculous." He stood up and paced the width of the room, hands behind his back. "No. No this is impossible, my friend. Something is doing this, something we cannot see."

The two men looked at the pictogram, worry etched

across their brows.

"Niaal, these findings cannot be right. There must be some corruption in the data, have them go back and check it again."

Niaal snapped his fingers and the pictogram was gone. "I already have. Three times. The findings are correct, Grefno." Niaal gestured, his hands empty. "I don't know what it is. I don't know how we can stop it."

Grefno held his head in hands, concentrating on his breathing. Niaal continued, his voice low and urgent. "If the predictions are correct, and I see no reason to doubt them, then the sickness will destroy us within three months. If it mutates, if it becomes airborne, then we have no hope at all. But if it is confinable and can be quarantined, then we need to consider forcibly moving the unaffected population to a place of safety. However, the farmland in the unaffected areas is next to useless. To avoid the prospect of famine we will need to expand into neighbouring territory. We will have no choice but to consider the annexation of lands belonging to the Prash-Romarians." He paused, seemingly appalled by his own words. "Or else we starve."

"What does the Mage know of this?" said Grefno. "The Mage knows everything."

Grefno snorted. "We both know that's not true. How much does he really know, seeing as how you're the only one he'll talk to these days?"

Niaal smiled. "Most of it. If he has some greater scheme, then he's playing his hand close to his chest. But for now it's fair to say he knows as much as anyone."

"The skirmishes along the borders have been getting worse of late," said Grefno, softly. "They have been antagonising us for months now. If we are forced to consider military action on a larger scale, not the petty border squabbles, but an actual invasion, then they may be better prepared to meet us than we would like. It's fair to say that relations between us and our neighbours have not been this bad since the Great War."

Niaal put a hand on his friend's shoulder. "The sickness could well kill us as soon as any war. The sickness is an enemy that cannot be fought. If a cure were to be found, then you and I would find it. If we could not then the Mage would, and yet we have nothing. Our best, only hope, is to set a course for military action against our neighbours, and hope that we might win for ourselves a place to live that is free from the sickness. I have taken the liberty of briefing General Vale, telling him to place his men in a state of readiness."

"I see. And if the sickness follows us?"

Niaal's smile stayed on his face, but his eyes betrayed horror. "We must be sure that it doesn't follow us. We must sterilise the whole region. We must leave nothing alive to follow in our wake."

Leah woke up, hungry. It was still dark outside. She lay there for ten minutes trying to will herself back to sleep, flicking her thoughts from happy ones to boring ones, but to no avail.

She got up and made her way downstairs, tiptoeing so as not to wake her mother, until she remembered. The house seemed suddenly cold and empty.

Taking a loaf of seed bread from the pantry, Leah cut herself a thick slice, and placed it on her favourite plate. It showed a Garden in summer, the porcelain beautifully painted. She smiled at the hairline cracks that spread across it, remembering when she'd dropped it as a child.

Leah had been so scared of telling her father, but he had merely smiled and told her not to worry.

"Anything can be mended," he'd said. "Anything. Plates are easy. Windows, cups, vases, easy to fix if you know how. Now, broken hearts, that's a different story altogether. Plates are easy compared to those."

She'd been puzzled at his words then, wondering how hearts could break, and was it the same as a broken arm, only inside? "Anything can be mended."

As she sat there munching in silence, she thought of the Garden, her Garden now. She thought of the soldiers and how they were getting on and, as she did so, her mind strayed to the woods outside the village. There was a stream that ran through it. She had caught minnows there as a child, wading out into the water with her dress tucked into her underclothes.

She sat bolt upright, suddenly wide-awake and instantly alert, her nerves on edge.

The Garden!

Before the illness, the Head Gardener had been working on a new irrigation scheme. The well in the town was running dry, and so he was trying to find new water supplies for the Garden, and the village itself. Leah had been at a meeting only a few days before the illness struck. As the only survivor, it was entirely possible she was the only person who knew of the scheme. With the town now cordoned off, a new local source of water was an urgent issue.

Alone in her bed, Leah felt the weight of responsibility threaten to crush her. There was no way she would be able to sleep now. So, throwing her clothes on over the top of her nightdress and grabbing the lantern by the door, she rushed out into the night.

Running down the street Leah heard the sounds of

footsteps, and remembered Krillan's orders just in time to duck into a doorway as a sentry passed the end of the road. If she had thought things through clearly she would have arranged an escort. It was official business, after all. But thankfully the soldier's hands were in his pockets, his head deep in thought as he ambled by, whistling a popular tune to himself.

Checking the coast was clear, Leah rushed towards the Garden. There were lights in the treetops. At least someone was still working. As she approached, she held up her palm and the gate swung obligingly open. There was nobody to challenge her. Leah felt unexpectedly cross with the guard for deserting his post and decided she'd tell someone when she reached...

The office door was open. At light was on inside.

It was happening again. Everyone was dead.

"Can I help you, Miss?"

She spun around. It was one of the militia. He was standing in the doorway, jacket off, shirt undone and a mug of hot tea in his hand. "You alright, Miss?"

"Yes. I was checking."

"Checking?"

"Checking things. You check things, don't you? For instance, I'm checking whether or not anyone is on guard duty. I strolled right in through the front door unchallenged. Could you explain how that happened?"

"We saw you on the monitors, Miss. With respect, Miss, you are actually in charge here. Although what you're doing out after curfew is anyone's guess."

A second guard came out of the office. "What's going on?"

"It's Miss Carleaf. She's checking things."

Leah straightened up. "Yes, thank you. I suddenly remembered that the sprouts in section three will need feeding, and hadn't left a note. I thought it best to pop over and tell the night shift myself."

"No need Miss, we'll call them from here. How much feed?"

"What?" Leah flustered. "Oh, er... three full units."

"Very good, Miss. Will there be anything else?"

"No." She turned to leave "Thank you, private."

"Welcome, Miss."

Leaving the guard hut, Leah made her way to the Head Gardener's offices. She hadn't spent much time here recently, despite the fact that by default she now was the Head Gardener. It felt too much like she was intruding.

The place was neat, tidy and ordered. She sat at the desk, flicking through papers. She found the notes relating to the irrigation scheme.

Whilst holding the sheet of paper, Leah noticed a small scribble on the bottom. A crude picture, badly drawn, showing some scaly creature, like a dragon, but without wings. A worm. Next to the drawing, stuck on the page, was a seed. It was one of the short hand messages Gardeners sometimes left for each other. Tiny dots of magic, they could hold instructions about weed killer or feed, growing tips or, more likely, rude messages and complaints.

It was the sort of thing only Gardeners knew about.

She licked her finger and brushed it against the seed, allowing the

psychoactive ink to penetrate her skin.

She felt herself floating, looking out through the eyes of someone else. With a start, she realised it was the Head Gardener. She was looking out though the eyes of a dead man, swimming through the memories left here on the paper.

Cold and unsettled by the sensation, she looked around.

She was in the town square. It was night, and the stars were shining overhead. She could smell wood smoke and... it smelt like beer. Beer and urine. She looked down to see that the Head Gardener was pissing against the wall of the town hall. It was, Leah accepted, a sensation she had never excepted to experience in her life. Feeling him zip himself up, Leah saw as the Gardener turned around and made his way across the market place. As he did so, she felt his heart race, felt him perspire as something crawled into the well. Something hideous, scaled and wet in the moonlight. It slid into darkness and out of sight like something from a nightmare.

The Gardener ran across to the well and looked down, but there was nothing there.

Whatever it had been it was gone.

With a cold snap, Leah fell out of the vision. Seed messages were usually no more than one or two words; simple pictograms. She'd never heard of anyone being able to construct one of such complexity. It was like she had actually been there, had actually been him.

She looked down at the picture on the sheet of paper. It was the same worm, the worm the Head Gardener had seen in the town square.

Leah felt suddenly exposed. Scared, she slipped the sheet of paper into her pocket. Drawing her coat around her shoulders, she went back to the guardroom and asked the guards to provide her with an escort safely home.

The creature would not attack him, of that Niaal was sure. Had he not, after all, raised it from an infant, nurtured it, given it food and a warm lair of its own? If the worm could speak, surely it would call him father.

Allesh was slowly coming under the creature's thrall. Already people were falling to the sickness as the worm tainted their water supply with its deadly excretions. Niaal considered this a fair sacrifice. For when the effects of the worm were felt through the whole of Inan, it would be he who would assume the mantle of ultimate power. It would be Niaal to which Inan turned to show them the way.

CHAPTER FOUR

The Alleshi Seventh Black Fleet possessed enough firepower to destroy a city. Invisible mermaids, creatures made of plasma and thought, sped through the water beside the ships, clearing the way of mines and other obstacles.

The Admiral sat cross-legged in the high backed leather chair in his quarters, his eyes closed in deep concentration. In his mind, he felt the waves of magical energy pour over him from the sphere he held in his hands. He could see the whole of Inan, spread before him.

There was a sharp rap on the door to his quarters, awakening him from his meditation. "Enter."

A senior officer ducked through the low bulkhead, and saluted. "Sir, urgent orders from the Castle. We are to make course at once to intercept the Prash-Romarian second fleet."

"Any idea as to why? I don't recall them straying into our waters recently."

"They're still over a hundred miles off. We have them on viewscopes now. The Castle have been shadowing them through spycraft."

The officer followed the Admiral as he climbed the ladder to the bridge. "Very well. Bring the image up ..." The words died in his throat as he stared in disbelief at the sight before him. He could see the thought image of the Prash-Romarian fleet hanging in the air in front of him. Ships were scattering. At least one had capsized, with two more obviously taking on water.

In the middle of the fleet there was a... thing. Vast, obscene, it was in every sense of the word impossible. It could not exist, and yet there it was. A sea creature, a magical beast, two miles long.

He watched in disbelief as it wrapped itself around the Prash-Romari flagship, crushing it like paper. Several smaller ships had opened fire, but it seemed to not even notice, the weapons harmlessly melting on the skin of the beast.

The comms officer on the bridge looked up, his face ashen. "It's magical in origin, sir. We don't know where it's getting that much power from, but it's taken everything they can throw at it!"

"Give me a line to the Prash-Romari Fleet!" snapped the Admiral.

There was a sound of static, then screams and then silence. They watched as ship after ship was smashed to pieces by the tentacles of the creature

"Sir?" the comms officer was looking to the Admiral. "Sir?"

The Admiral snapped himself out of shock. "Fighters to immediate launch. I want them armed with Bright Sun charges. Reach the area and destroy that thing.

"Contact the masters of our nearest ships and tell them to stand to pick up any survivors. Tell them to dump their cargoes to make better speed. They will be fully reimbursed at the current market price on reaching harbour, plus an additional handling charge. Please remind them that they are bound my maritime law to comply with this request."

"Sir."

From the flight deck, fast attack fighters silently fell up into the sky, their deadly cargo slung beneath. Like a swarm of flies eager for the feast of a corpse, they made their way toward the Prash-Romari vessels.

Turning his back on the carnage, he prepared to send a communiqué to his superiors in the Castle. If this was magical warfare, then it was on an unprecedented scale, and the sooner he made his report the safer he would feel. Not that the word 'safe' had any meaning compared to the size and power of the attack he had just witnessed. Bracing himself, he composed his message.

Outside the village, the patrol on the roadblock was clearly bored. The guards were sitting on fuel drums, playing cards. Despite the highly inflammable symbols on them, one or two were smoking.

The wood was in sight. She was in half a mind to just walk through them and smile, and see if they challenged her or not. But no.

Three days ago a farmer had gone through a border point in pursuit of a fugitive cow that had wandered away from his farm. He was just going to get his cow and bring it back, and no one need ever know or worry.

A boy with a high velocity impulse projector had drilled him through the head from 500 yards. He was still lying there. There was no news of what had happened to the cow.

Moving back along the road Leah took a left turn and headed down the lane that sprung out at ninety degrees to the main road. It was no more than a track used by farm vehicles. Trees grew out of the high hedgerows that bordered it, as it made its way up a small valley. There was no sign of roadblocks here, at least.

Turning the corner, Leah saw a transport drawn up across the road. Two soldiers sat on the roof, listening intently to a radio set.

She turned back before they saw her and started to ask awkward questions. Heading back up to the road that led to the village she passed a field of maize. It was ready for harvest, and stood over twelve feet high. It looked easy enough to hide in. There was a chance that she could simply walk through it, following the lines of the tractors, and never be seen.

The only problem was how she would know if there were already soldiers in the field, though. Slinging her bag over her shoulder, Leah jumped and caught a branch of a nearby oak. From her vantage point half way up the tree she could see that there was no one to be seen in the maize and no sign of movement.

She took a piece of rope from her bag and fashioned it into a crude leash, and held it tightly. If challenged she would say her dog had run off and she was chasing after it. It wasn't the best plan in the world, but it would have to do.

Taking a deep breath, Leah turned into the field, following the path left by farm machinery. Every twenty paces she stopped dead, and listened for the sound of rustling, but nothing came. If there were soldiers in the field with her they were probably as blind as she was. The thought of this cheered her up immeasurably. Unless they had heat-seeking visor-ware and had smart mined the area. The thought of this depressed her immeasurably.

Workers from the Garden had enhanced the corn in the field. She herself had worked on its construction as an apprentice. It stood some fifteen feet high, with ears the size of cats. It could be matured in a fortnight, and was rich in energy and vitamins. Magically force grown, it was just one of the everyday marvels that the Gardeners and Sages were responsible for.

Leah looked around, trying to get her bearings. She had travelled west since leaving the road, but she had no idea which way was which, now that she was in the field. Deciding that she must be at least half way there and it was as dangerous to go back as to go forward, she broke into a gentle jog and headed on down the tractor marks.

She emerged near a small stream, which she followed uphill further, until she found herself back on the road, although well beyond the cordoned area.

"Well. That was easy." She smiled as she headed to her grandma's house.

Leah's grandmother had married three times, each time to a wonderful man, although each very different to the others. The first was her childhood sweetheart, Leah's paternal grandfather, who had been killed in active service while still in his late teens. Widowed young, and with a child to think of, she next married a gentle, educated man, who was a teacher in the village school. He had been loved by everyone, and it was a tragedy felt by the whole community when he drowned one summer, whilst saving the life of a small boy who had fallen into a lake. Her third husband was a farmer, himself recently widowed. The two of them had enjoyed what time they had together until he too simply passed away in his sleep one night. Leah's grandmother had decided that three husbands had been enough. For now at least.

The old lady answered the door in her apron, flour up to her elbows.

"Leah! Oh my dear, it's so good to see you! They've lifted the cordon then, have they?"

Leah smiled sheepishly. "Afraid not, Gran. But I was worried sick about you, and wasn't going to let some boys with guns stop me."

"Stop you?" Her grandmother looked taken aback. "Leah, you could have been killed!" She hugged Leah, and then pulled back sharply. "You're not carrying the contagion are you?"

Leah blushed. "I was passed fit by the hospital last night. I took a diagnostic stick with me on the way out, and stuck it in before I knocked. Look." She held up her wrist. A small purple light blinked back at her. "See? Clear as a bell." She hung back. "Of course, if you'd prefer I went –"

Leah's grandma smiled. "If you're dying, then we'd better put the kettle on first and have a slice of cake. Besides, no one has come right out and said how the illness is transmitted, anyway. The news channels have been vague, to say the least."

"Thanks Granny. You haven't got a man in the house or anything, have you?"

"Why, love? You desperate?"

Leah pulled a face at the thought of sudden desperate sex with the kind of polite, wrinkly and distinctly elderly gentleman her grandmother associated with. "Euuw! No. Er... I mean 'Euuw, no thanks I've just had one?'"

Leah went straight to the bookshelf and started pulling books out; her father's old books, stored here since he died. "I've been trying to call you for days. The comms are down all over the village. I expect it's the same everywhere."

"No, we're fine. It's just you, apparently, and the area around the Castle. We still get everything fine. News reports, weather, all the usual bulletins. In fact, everything outside the village is the same as it ever was." She flicked a finger at the wall, stopping a light entertainment music show she had been enjoying.

"You mean apart from the sickness, of course?"

"There is no sickness out here. It's only been reported

as being in the village and a few other isolated places."

"Really?" said Leah suddenly puzzled. "How odd. I wonder why they think we need to be cut off from the rest of the world in that case?"

"You mean apart from the fact that you might be carrying some kind of end-of-civilisation-as-we-know-it plague thingy?"

Leah sat on the chair by the bookshelf, her hands flicking through pages. "I know we've all been calling it 'The Contagion', but I'm not sure it is. Contagious, I mean. I don't know how you get it, but I don't think it's person to person contact, somehow. And besides, you don't get diseases through comms lines."

"Not usually, no. What is it you're looking for, anyway?"

Leah carried on reading, not looking up. "Came to see you, Gran. I was worried."

"I'm the one that should be worried. So, what is it you're looking for?"

Leah smiled, holding up a thick volume; pages thin as tissue paper. "This. Dad's book on rare beasts. He was always going on about them. I'd look it up electronically, but the system's been down for days now. Whatever it is that they want to contain, they're doing their best to stop us finding out too much about it. Can't imagine why."

Leah continued flicking through the book until she came to the entry on Worms. There were many types, some large, some small, some ridiculously so.

"What's that you've found?" said Gran, bringing her a hot drink. "Worms? Filthy creatures. You came all this way, risking life and limb, to look at a book on worms?"

"I came all this way risking, as you say, life and limb, to make sure you were well. But yes, to read this book. The village library doesn't have this volume. I know, because I checked. Look –" she held the book open at a page. It showed an ugly looking creature with a revolting carapace, not unlike the beast she had seen in her vision of the well. "This one here? I saw something like it the other night, I'm sure of it."

Taking the book from her Leah's grandma slid some spectacles down over her nose. "Soft Worm. This what you think you saw? A Soft Worm?"

"Yes. Well, no I'm not entirely certain, but it's a close enough match. The eyes weren't quite the same, the head different in coloration. But yes, I'd say that was what I'd seen."

"Soft Worm. Vegetarian, that's good. Not venomous. Likes the dark, usually timid except when young are threatened. Secretes many chemicals prized for their medicinal purposes, of particular value to the wizarding community, although use is limited to those of extreme high standing." Their eyes met. "Do you think this thing belongs to the Mage? It might have escaped."

Leah studied the picture again. "It's possible, I suppose. In which case I imagine he'd be very keen to get it back again. Even so, it still doesn't look quite the same as the one here. You don't suppose it's some new species do you?"

"Unlikely. More likely it's a mutant, some wretched product of gene splicing perhaps. Either way, I don't think it will do anyone any good having it wandering around the village."

Leah carried on reading. The Soft Worm was reckoned to be prized by herbalists. Among its many qualities were the secretions given off by glands located in the mouth. They were renowned for their healing properties by the wizards of Southern Praal.

If this thing was a Soft Worm, Leah thought, then her

grandma could be right. It might have escaped from the Castle, and Leah might be richly rewarded for bringing it back. Who knows what really went on in the domain of the Mage, after all.

"I should go." Leah said. "Are you sure you'll be alright?"

"I'll be fine, my love. Whatever it is that's making you people ill, it doesn't seem to like the other side of the river." She put some cakes into Leah's bag. "So who are you going to tell about this thing then?"

"There's a captain of the militia they've put in the Garden with us. Bloody man's a nuisance, but I suppose I'll have to report it to him, see if his men can't catch it."

Leah's grandmother gathered her up in a tight hug.

"Leah, be careful how you phrase it. If this creature does belong to the Mage then he could be very grateful. Very grateful indeed. You need to make sure that some of that gratitude goes your way. Do you follow me?"

Leah smiled. She knew exactly what Gran meant. This was her chance to shine, her chance to prove that she had so much more to offer than being a mere Gardener. Although she was acting Head Gardener, as soon as the current crisis resolved itself the Castle would formally appoint a new head. One with the right qualifications and formal magical training, no doubt. But if she could make something of herself here, then she could be legitimately running the Gardens for real, like her father before her.

"May I take this book with me, please?"

"You may. Just don't tell anyone where you got it from, there's a good girl, eh?"

Making her way back to her house, Leah changed clothes before going to the hospital to check on her mother.

Glora was sitting by the bedside as she arrived. She was holding Saran's hand through the thin plastic sheeting that formed her isolation cube, oxygen gently hissing through the filtered pumps below her bed. She was reading a book with her free hand, but looked up at Leah and smiled gently as she entered the room. Leah took Saran's hand from her and slid into the chair by the bed, now warm from where Glora had been sitting.

"How is she?"

"Why don't you ask her yourself? She's looking much better." Glora smiled at her friend, lying so pale and still in the bed.

She looked worse, of course, but Leah appreciated the comment anyway. She picked up her mother's hand and sat there, listening to the sound of her breathing.

Glora gave Leah a kiss on the forehead and was gone.

Her mother would pull through this. It was bad enough to have lost her father when she was little. To lose her mother now was... well, it wouldn't be right.

She looked at Saran. She took after her mother in her looks, as much as she matched her father in temperament. Everyone has to say goodbye to their parents at some point, Leah reasoned. It was the way of things.

But not like this, not now. Saran was so full of life, so kind and funny, and gentle, and she shouldn't have to go like this. Taken by some wretched disease.

There was always a cure. That was what the Garden was for.

She touched her wrist, opening a line to the Garden. The central computer fed her updates of the work that had taken place today. The watering, pruning, the spores harvested. No disasters, no calamities. Things were going as smoothly as ever.

The Mage. He would find an answer; all he needed were the right materials.

The Mage would save them. The Mage would save Saran.

Leah made her way to the Inn. With the town under martial law, opening times were severely limited, and so enthusiastic drinkers like Gim and Rendolph had to double their efforts to make sure they kept their good name with each other, and bad reputation with the rest of the townsfolk.

Across the market square she saw Krillan's men. They had stopped a family on a cart and were searching it. She saw Sergeant Wallas look at her guiltily. The blockade around the town was tight as could be, but all the same, the military still insisted on these spot checks now and then. It was supposed to reassure people, let them know that someone had taken a firm hand and things were under control. In actuality, they served no purpose at all. The sickness wasn't going to be hiding in a cartload of milk churns. And besides, it wasn't as if they had been able to leave the village and surrounding areas, anyway.

This was just Krillan playing at soldiers. Being seen to be in control, letting the people know who was in charge around here. It was pointless. One of the soldiers accidentally knocked a milk churn from the back of the wagon, and it fell clattering to the cobbles. The milk poured out and along the gulley that ran down the middle of the street. The farmer looked furious, but said nothing. Leah stood, wondering how the soldiers would react, but they merely looked ashamed as they picked the churn up and put it back on the wagon. Sergeant Wallas wrote something on a piece of paper and handed it to the man.

"Here. Take this to the Estate Office in the morning, and you'll be fully reimbursed. Sorry about that."

The man took it from him, his face like thunder. "Just doing your job," he said stiffly.

"I don't know what we're doing," said Wallas, catching Leah's eye across the road. "I don't know anything that's going on these days. I think the whole world's going mad."

There was a sudden brightness around them, and everyone looked up. The sky was ablaze, like another sun had briefly risen, and set again.

"What was that?" said the farmer.

"Don't know," said Wallas, touching his wrist-port, hoping for information. But none came. "Who knows what's happening now?"

"That looked like an explosion." Leah called. "It did, didn't it? A very large explosion, but a long way off."

"Nothing we're aware off," said Wallas. He turned to the farmer. "On your way now. And again, my sincere apologies for the accident. If you have any trouble tell them to talk to me and I'll sort it out at once." He turned to Leah. "You too, Miss."

"The curfew's not called just yet, Sergeant."

"No, Miss. But it's not safe being on the streets these days." He looked at his own men, crossly. "Can't tell what might happen."

"Sergeant, that was an explosion. You know it was."

"I didn't hear anything, Miss."

"Magical weaponry doesn't need to make a sound. Are we are at war, Sergeant?"

"Miss, if I knew, I'd say you would too. Not an easy thing to keep quiet, a war."

"No. No, I suppose not."

"Who knows what it means. So many weird things happening, why should one more be any the odder?"

With a backward glance at the sky, Leah made her way to the inn. Her two friends waved to her as she entered, ducking her head below the low wooden beams.

"Leah! You're just in time. More cider, barman!"

"No. Thank you, but no."

"More mead, barman, one for the lady."

"No, really, I'm fine."

"Really really?"

She smiled. "Oh, alright. But make it a large one."

"There we go. Hey, how's your mum? Any news?"

Leah took a huge swig of the sweet honeyed drink and sat down on the worn varnished bench next to them.

"They say she's stabilised. Which means she's dying, but it won't be tonight. They don't know what it is, do they? They haven't got a clue what they're doing. There are people falling down ill all over the place and they haven't the first inkling of what's wrong."

Rendolph banged his glass down on the table.

"Well the Mage must be doing something. I mean, it's not like he runs the whole country or anything, not your actual day to day running, but he must know what's going on, right? And here we are right on his doorstep. We're not some little village out in the middle of nowhere, are we?"

"It's a bit like that," said Gim. "Only worse. We're right next to the Castle and yet they ignore us."

"The Mage will think of something," said Leah. "It's what he does. He thinks of things. Holds back our enemies, cares for us, sustains us all with his power."

The boys looked at each other, worried.

"I know you're under stress, love, but you haven't suddenly got religion have you?"

"No."

"Can happen."

"He's a Mage. He's not a god."

Gim knocked back his drink in one. "No. Be better if he was. We could pray to him at least. Other countries, their Mages appear in public you know."

"Bollocks they do." Rendolph said.

"They do. Some countries the Mage speaks about things, not like ours, stuck up there in that Castle of his. I mean, don't get me wrong; I like what he does. If it weren't for him then we'd have all sorts making their way here. We'd have war again. And whatever happens I don't want a war. Poncing round like your man Krillan, shining his boots so he can see up ladies' skirts."

"Good idea, though."

"Bloody good idea."

"I need your help, boys," Leah said. "I think there's something in the well. A creature."

"Of course there is," said Gim. "It's a magical wishing well, isn't it?"

"That's right," said Rendolph. "Leah looked in it and wished she could find the best-looking lads in the world. Good looking, sophisticated, witty." Rendolph belched. "Well mannered, and with bollocks the size of jibber fruit."

Leah sighed. "That's as may be, but would you stop talking with them for one minute and let me finish?"

Gim and Rendolph exchanged mock hurt looks. "Oooh."

"Stop it. Will you help me?"

"Well, of course we will. We always do. But tell me,

why we should. Just to put my mind at ease."

Leah smiled, her hands folded on her lap. "Three reasons. Firstly, if I'm right, then it might earn us the gratitude of the Mage. He might be able to help my mother."

"We've already said we'll do it," said Gim.

"Secondly, it might make us rich."

"I already liked it," said Rendolph. "Like it more now."

"How will it make us rich?" Gim said.

"If we find the creature, and the Mage feels generous, he might reward us. You could get a promotion out of it."

"Fair enough," said Rendolph. "You said three things, though."

Leah knocked half of her drink back, burped, and said "And thirdly, if you do help us I'll get drunk and get my tits out before last orders tonight."

Gim and Rendolph slapped hands in the air in mock delight. "Right, that's your lot!" shouted the barman. "Time to go."

"Oh dear," said Leah, smiling at the boys. "Still, two out of three's not bad is it?"

"Which two?" said Gim.

"My lady lumps are staying where they are, thank you very much. You'll have to settle for fame, fortune and the eternal gratitude of the government."

"So what is it you want us to do?" said Rendolph.

As the three friends left the inn, Leah told them her plan. And as she did so, the colour slowly drained from their drink-flushed cheeks.

"You in then?" asked Leah.

"I'm in," said Gim. "Anything for a laugh."

"Actually.... Actually, no." said Rendolph. "Sorry. But I don't think I can."

"Oh, come on," said Gim. "You've got to."

"No he doesn't," said Leah. "Not if he doesn't want to. Besides, it makes more sense to leave someone up top in case anything goes wrong."

"Hold on! What's with this 'In case things go wrong' business?" spluttered Gim.

Leah smiled. "It will make us rich. We split it three ways. Gim and I go down the well, Rendolph waits up top."

"That's very generous of you," said Gim.

"It's very generous of you too," said Rendolph. "It's a three-way split."

"I know," said Gim. "It's still generous, though."

CHAPTER FIVE

Night in the village came, as always, with the last rays of the sun catching the towers of the Castle, which reflected them back and then held them with a soft turquoise luminescence. As the last rays fell behind the hill, the shadows lengthened and spread over the timber framed houses, along the cobbled streets and over the rooftops. The thatch of the cottages turned a deep russet, sparkling with the silver from the sat dishes and aerials poking up from the smoking chimney pots. The air hung heavy with the scent of burning peat and turf, as rich as whiskey.

Here and there lights began to twinkle as streetlamps were illuminated or people lit lanterns. At times of festival, or in summer, the night could be as vibrant as day in the town, with folks wandering from tavern to tavern, mingling with the hustle and bustle of traders selling snacks and beverages that you'd never want in daylight, or when sober.

Tonight the town was nearly silent. The only sound was of the occasional patrol of a militia guard, or of children being called indoors.

As the sky turned from dark blue to black, the last ray of sunlight caught an aircraft, high overhead. It turned deep silver, bright white like a pearl, and then, as darkness claimed even the highest reaches, it vanished altogether, save the odd twinkling of navigational lights.

Inside her house Leah sat in the kitchen, her hands folded on her lap. She was dressed in dark clothes, and had a scarf pulled tight around her head. On the table was a satchel and some snap lights, small disposable emergency lights she had taken from work. Gim would be here any second. She took a book out of the satchel and flicked though it, returning to the page which showed the creature she had glimpsed the other night. She had read it fifty times since that night and knew most of it by heart.

Soft Worm. Harmless, highly prized. She slipped her father's book back into her bag anyway.

She had spent the evening at her mother's bedside. There had been no change in her condition, which meant that she was not getting any worse at least. But she was getting no better. Those people who had been brought in to the hospital that first week, like her mother, had either died after a couple of days, or had stabilised and were now just lying there. It seemed that the sickness either claimed you outright, or else left you sat there. In the larder.

The thought slapped her across her face. Larder? What a strange thought. It was like the disease was eating them, but it was full for the moment, and so had left the other sick people alone while it slept off its feast.

There was a knock at the door.

"You ready, then?" It was Gim, a large bag slung over his shoulder. Leah nodded and slipped outside, pulling the door behind her.

"I take it the patrols haven't seen you?" she whispered, her eyes darting about the deserted night time street.

"There were loads down by the inn, but they've all gathered together for something. I think it's a works party. There'll be speeches, more speeches, and some poor bugger will end up with a plaque to hang on his wall telling the whole world how he was stuck in the same job for most of his adult life."

"Come on then. Let's do it. Where's Rendolph?"

"I'm here," said Rendolph, slipping in behind Gim. "Sure you want to go through with this?"

"No," said Leah. "But we'll do it anyway. You just make sure that no one takes the ladder away while we're down there."

The three friends made their way along the street, cautiously trying to keep to the shadows and doorways as much as they could. They passed by the entrance to the market square, looking this way and that for any sign of Captain Krillan's militiamen, but there was neither sight nor sound of them.

Gim hosted the bag higher up his shoulder.

"You think this is a good idea?"

"What?" said Rendolph. "No, of course I'm not sure. I think this is lunacy, and I think you're a madman for agreeing to go with her."

They sprinted across the square, taking refuge by the side of the well.

Gim pulled a wire ladder from his bag and began to feed it down into the darkness. It fell with a reassuring clatter at the bottom, meaning that the ladder was at least longer than the hole was deep.

"Who goes first then?"

Leah took one of the snap lights from her belt and dropped it into the gloom. As it hit the bottom they were able to see the brick walls of the well, and the dry floor. Gim looked at her, quizzically. "I thought we wanted to find this thing, not scare it off."

"We do. But I don't want anything to scare me off first." Leah looked down into the well. "I'll go first. Come on, before the guards come back."

"What do we do if they find the ladder?" said

Rendolph.

"I don't know. I suppose they'll either come down after us, or else they'll wait at the top for us. All we can do is hope they don't find us first."

"Here," said Rendolph. "You'll need this." He passed Gim a small silver hipflask and an earthenware bottle. "Brandy. Just in case they haven't got a bar down there. Drop of cider too. Worst case, you could always knock yourself up a pint of snakebite."

"Snakebite. That's very funny, that," said Gim, slipping the drink into his bag. "You're a funny man, Rendolph."

Leah made her way down the ladder. Years of working on the higher branches of the Garden had taught her and Gim to move quickly up and down all manner of ropes and swings, and the pair of them had no real fear of falling.

Although the worm was supposed to be harmless, facing wild animals was something Leah had little experience of, so she had brought with her a shepherd's crook that had for many years sat above the bar in the tavern. Leah had some vague idea of using it to hold the beast at bay in case it should prove frisky. She also carried, slung over her shoulder, a couple of insecticide pumps, filled with a compound of her own making. A powerful sedative, it was used by vets to put horses to sleep before operating on them. She had made the dose twice as strong. She hoped that if she had to use it, it would be powerful enough to put the beast to sleep without killing it in the process. The compound was fairly straightforward in manufacture, being a mixture of the stamen of two flowers grown in the Garden. Botany students were known to spike each other's drinks with it, sending each other into instant slumber; a practice which had had been frowned on in recent years, although it was known to still continue.

They reached the bottom and stood there, listening to the echoes of their breathing in the darkness. The well had been dry for many months, but the floor was still wet with soft mud. In front of them was a hole in the wall, three feet high and perfectly round. Gim backed away from it.

"Is that its burrow? It must have teeth like shovels."

Leah leaned forward, to closer examine the hole. "It must also be very clever, these walls are constructed from brick." Gim looked at her puzzled. "It's a feeder tunnel, brings water in from the reservoir, wherever that is. It's part of the well system. Come on, our creature must have gone through here, and so that means we're going after it."

"Hold on, let's send this ahead." Gim said, taking something from his bag. He held up a small mechanical figure of a man, some ten inches high. It was made entirely of brass.

"You took one of the Pixies from the gates at work?" Leah said, in a mildly disapproving tone.

Gim smiled. "Might have."

"That's a sackable offence, straight up."

"Who's going to sack me? You?" He set the Pixie on the ground and clicked the on switch on its back. A small burst of purple magic swam around its head. Gim took a small pen-shaped instrument from the creature's chest and slid it into his wrist-port. His eyes glowed briefly purple.

"Hello," squeaked the Pixie, in a mechanical approximation of Gim's voice.

"Off you go then," said Gim, one eye now closed. He could now see through two sets of eyes. One were his own, the other were the Pixie's, giving him a dizzying view that soon cleared once he and Leah swam out of sight. In his mind he could see and hear all that the Pixie could.

"Right. We're off."

"That was good thinking, actually," said Leah. "I'm impressed."

"We used to use them all the time when we had that trouble with fungal growth in the higher branches. It was safer than sending a botanist up a ladder when you weren't sure it'd take the weight. They're quite easy to use once you get the hang of them," said Gim, promptly walking straight into a wall.

"I'm sure they are."

"Just finding my feet. Not as easy as it looks, this. It's alright, just give me a moment." He paused, concentrating. "Right, there's a large chamber twenty feet ahead of us. Nothing there he can see, and he's using IR and sonar. Come on."

Leah followed him through the darkness, reassured that there was nothing waiting for them. They came out into a large chamber, as Gim had said they would. The Pixie was waiting for them; the tiny LEDs in its eyes blinking in the darkness. Gim wobbled on his feet again as the construct looked at him. "Whoa, there we go again. Look away, little lad, look away."

The chamber had a high roof suggesting that it had been part of the original reservoir for the village, laid down many years before. Leah massaged her wrist, hoping to check their position with central data, but found only static. They were too far underground already, shielded by the tons of earth and rock above them.

Gim waited until the Pixie had set off down the tunnel opposite them before attempting to walk again.

"And you're absolutely certain this is safe?"

"Nothing's certain in life, Gim. But if my father's books

are right, and they do tend to be, then this Soft Worm thing is quite passive. Ugly, but passive." Leah slapped him on the back. "Come on. Let's keep moving."

Together the two of them followed the mechanical construct into the dark, their footsteps echoing eerily along the narrow wet passage.

They turned the corner, took one hesitant look behind them, and then disappeared into the blackness.

Grefno sat in a green leather armchair in the Great Library of the Castle, forty-five feet up, a lamp held in mid-air before him by a swarm of tiny brass butterflies that kept it aloft using their mechanical wings. The platform was a favourite of his, being as it was between the disciplines of science and ethics, a crossroads at the worlds of 'can we?' and 'yes, but should we?' It was bright and airy, and yet musty and secretive enough to appeal to him. He had been coming here to read ever since the Castle's doors were first opened in the heady days following the end of war. It was one of his special places.

The library was theoretically available via wrist-port to everyone. And yet Grefno preferred to use the books themselves. To feel the crispness of the dry paper, to smell the musty spines of the leather-bound volumes; that was really the only way to truly access the library. It was the mark of a true wizard to take time to actually read the book.

Grefno was reading a history of diplomatic relations, with special mention of advice on enduring times of hardship and plague. Not exactly light reading, and once or twice he had felt his eyelids droop and his head nod.

Were it not for the fact that sitting on a chair forty-five feet up in the air was not necessarily the safest place in the world to be, he may well have fallen asleep completely.

He looked up from his study to see Niaal, rising towards him on the mechanical stair lift. The circular iron platform took him in ever-higher circles until he was level with the platform where Grefno was sitting. He stepped from the platform neatly, acknowledging his friend with a nod as he dropped an electronic file on Grefno's lap. It was a sheet of plastic that contained an animated 3D image, responding to the touch of Grefno's hand as he manipulated the pictures and information on the page.

Grefno looked up from the map in shock. "You're sure about this?"

"I am. I wish that it were not so, my friend, but the facts speak plainly. The other Sages are in agreement with me." Niall sat down beside his friend, pulling a small stool from under a polished wooden table. "There is no cure, Grefno. According to my research, the sickness cannot be stopped. It can only be contained. It is the best we can hope for. Soon it may well be airborne, and from then on we have no hope. Our allies will not aid us, we have no course of action open to us, except escape."

"And the Mage? What does he say? Has any attempt been made to contact the other Mages on Inan? Surely Ramus-Bey himself must realise that this could soon be sweeping out over the rest of Bethel? This is a global problem. Do they have nothing to say on the subject?"

Niaal turned away, his eyes on the myriad colours of the book spines arranged along the walls of the library as far as the eye could see.

"The other Mages have not spoken on the issue yet. It may be that they could find a way out, but while they ponder, our people are sick and dying. We must act and act now." Niaal drew a circle in the air, showing the geographical presentation of the state. "We must sterilise the entire area. The Castle will be forfeit, and the Mage moved to a place of safety. This whole region will be uninhabitable for generations to come, a dead zone."

"But this is the Garden, this green, fertile crescent is where the produce of four fifths of the entire state's foodstuff comes from. If we lose this, then our people will surely starve. Without the psychoactive plants, then we will be unable to create the necessary magical weaponry to defend ourselves. We are a small nation. We are reliant on the plants from the Garden for our protection." Grefno said.

"Our neighbours have land, good land to spare. They will not give it to us freely. For the sake of our own survival we must be prepared to take it from them."

Grefno sat in heavy silence. "There must be another way. We are not without friends, and should give good account of ourselves, but surely it must be in everyone's interest to maintain the stability that has lasted these past fifteen years?"

Niaal shrugged. "Ever since the collapse of the larger Bethel, individual breakaway republics have been vying for position. There are many smaller nation states that would take advantage of our misfortune. What other choice do we have? Sit here and wait for the disease to eat us all? Grefno, you must know what is happening out there. Our own people in the Castle are no longer safe. How long before our guards go down with it? How long before you or I succumb?"

Grefno stiffened. "I would give my life ten times over if need be, for my country."

Niaal faced him squarely, his eyes full of sorrow. "And

how long before it takes the Mage, even?"

Grefno's face froze. It didn't even bear thinking about. He stood up, smoothing his robes. At once his entourage of warriors surrounded, him, gliding down ladders from the platforms where they had been watching in secret while the two Sages talked. Grefno nodded to his friend and began the climb down towards the main staircase. Around him small mechanical gnomes blinked in the dusty light and burrowed back into the bookshelves, ordering and cataloguing as they went. Grefno saw one go, diving into the woodwork, and was reminded of how, as a boy, he had seen a bird chase a worm in his garden. He paused, quite taken aback by the sudden unexpected memory. He had been four or five, and had been playing at being a farmer. He had dug a section of dry earth under the apple tree, and made furrows with a spoon. He had deposited breakfast cereal into the rows, and was about to water it in the hope that it would grow. His brother had come out of the kitchen and laughed at him cruelly, but he was adamant that the cereal would grow, when he saw the bird fly down and take the worm.

Grefno paused, suddenly lost in the memory. As a Sage,. he was so immersed in the pharmacological tools at his disposal that his subconscious would, from time to time, become open to influences and patterns that others wouldn't so readily see. What was it telling him? Was his brother connected in some way?

Grefno's brother had joined the navy as a youth and had risen to the rank of admiral before retiring. He was now living in the mountains, surrounded by his grandchildren, who adored him and believed him to be a great conjuror.

Or the bird. What if the sickness was avian in origin? How in the fifty-nine hells would you contain a virus that was spread by migrating wildfowl? It didn't bear thinking about.

Clearly, in his mind, he still saw it. The bird chasing the worm.

Grefno blinked twice, and the image was gone.

*

Captain Krillan came out of the hut by the roadside and looked up at the sky. It was cold and there was a faint chill coming from the east. He drew his collar tighter. Lights approached along the road and he felt a rush of professional satisfaction as the transport was challenged by his militiamen. It was a military vehicle, regular infantry. At once Krillan felt his hackles rise. They always looked down on his men as hobbyists, amateurs, never realising the worth in what they did.

The militiamen saluted as a tall figure emerged from the transport. Krillan snapped to attention.

"General Vale! What an unexpected pleasure!"

"It's the middle of the night and we're freezing our knackers off," grunted the General, acknowledging Krillan with the slightest of salutes. "Hardly a pleasure for either of us. Let's go inside. I've got news for you."

Krillan followed him into the hut. A small heater burned in the corner of the room, giving out a pitiful warmth that vanished as soon as it touched your skin. The privilege that came with rank.

General Vale sat down on the only chair. "This bloody disease, then. How are we getting on?"

"The cordon is being enforced around the village, sir. My men are controlling all traffic on the roads and refusing entry in or out."

"Good. And the curfew?"

"In place as of seven nights ago. We haven't had anything we can't handle yet. The men have been told to shoot if need be."

The General rubbed the bridge of his nose between his thumb and forefinger, looking for a second like the tired old man he was. "And do you think we need a curfew, Captain?"

"I think it prudent, Sir. We need to control movement if we wish to contain the sickness and, as you know, everything is that much harder in the dark. Seemed to me to be the simplest solution was restrict movement after sunset."

The General leaned forward in the chair. "I think we're all blundering about in the dark here, Captain. No one knows what this thing is or where it came from, and no one has the slightest idea how to stop it. Last thing we need is people running round like headless chickens. You've heard the news about the Prash-Romari fleet, I take it?"

"We heard reports, Sir. We all have. I mean, the explosion lit up the sky even here." Krillan paused. "I believe it's being officially passed off as atmospheric disturbance."

"You're doing a good job, Captain. All the right people are noticing. But you're going to have to take a bit more on board, I'm afraid. Army command is gearing up for something big. Obviously I'm not going into the details and nor would you expect me to." He fixed a clear gaze on Krillan. "I'm telling you all this because you shan't be coming with us, Captain."

"Sir, I've proven myself time and again. If there's something going on then I want to be there, be a part of it, not stuck here checking peasant's wagons."

"I appreciate that, Captain. But please believe me when

I say that your work here is considered vital. All regular troops that can be spared are being shipped out at first light, as quietly as we can manage it. We will, of course, be needing to pull extra resources from the hospitals in readiness in case things get... well. Things could get complicated, Captain."

Krillan stood stiffly, his fingernails biting into his hands behind his back. His whole adult life he head dreamed of going into action, and now when it looked as if there was finally to be some chance of adventure, he was to stay here, guarding farmers and shopkeepers in the shadow of the Castle. His face burned with shame. The General stood up slowly, Krillan snapping to attention as he did so.

"That will be all Captain. Carry on."

Krillan watched Vale leave, the transport pulling away into the dark. He stood there, silently seething, too wound up to sleep now.

"Sergeant!" he barked into the mess tent. "Have the men mustered for patrol. Armed and ready in five minutes."

"Yes Sir."

If Krillan were forced to sit out a war stuck here, then he would do so to the very best of his abilities.

The ground had become increasingly wet underfoot the further they travelled from the well, so much so that it was now splashing around their ankles as they walked. Leah remembered the Head Gardener and his scheme to find a new water supply.

"How far have we come?" said Gim.

"About a mile. I would have thought we'd have seen something by now. A nest or something. Droppings, that kind of thing."

"Great. The inn is open, there's a chair with my name on it and a flagon of cold beer on the table in front of it, and I'm down here with you looking for monster poo. In my spare time."

"Oh, but you love it."

"I do not."

"You do too."

"I still seriously do not."

"You still seriously do."

They stood there, looking at the walls of the tunnel. "Who do you think built these?" said Leah, running her hand along them. "You would have thought that someone would have made a big thing of it, really."

Gim stopped to look with her. "Why?" He asked, feeling the smoothness of the cold rock.

"Well. You know, big job like this, man in charge – and trust me, it's always a man – he'd expect recognition. He'd want a bottle of wine and a round of applause. He'd probably want a school named after him at the very least. Seems strange that none of us have ever heard of him."

"Or her."

"No, really, it's a man."

"How can you tell?"

Leah smiled at Gim, who was suddenly not smiling back at her. His face was white, his eyes huge as he stared at her... No, not at her, he was looking over her shoulder.

"It's behind me, isn't it?"

"Uh... yes."

"Big?"

"I... think I might've wet myself."

Leah slowly turned around. Behind her, something huge was moving. Something that was slowly sliding towards them in the darkness.

Leah slid the spray gun from her backpack and primed it.

The worm was thirty feet long from tip to tail. It pulled itself along the ground on four powerful looking limbs, armed with claws. The creature hissed softly at them, its tongue flicking in the air, as if smelling prey. Which, as Leah quickly realised, was something it shouldn't be doing if it were indeed vegetarian.

Leah backed away towards Gim, slipping the other spray from her shoulder, and handing it to him.

"When I say so, let him have it in the face. He can't hurt us, but it's big, so we need to keep back in case he falls on us. You ready?"

"No."

"Good. One, two, THREE!"

The sprays shot out an acrid purple mist into the beast's face.

The creature reared its head. Leah raised the spray gun and let it have another dose. She saw it clearly hit the worm full in the nostrils. She watched as it did not pass out, did not fall asleep, and most certainly did not fall over and start snoring. A hideous tongue flitted out and licked the liquid from its face. If anything, it liked it, and wanted more.

"I thought you said that would stop it?"

"I did. It should have. Maybe I mixed it wrong. Maybe it's too weak or something."

The creature slid across the tunnel, weaving from side to side, as it tasted the air with its tongue. Gim pulled an emergency flare from his belt, and pulled the pin from the top. At once it created a fierce orange flame. He waved it in the air, hoping the light might frighten it away. Indeed, the creature slunk back away from it, but as it did so it hissed, loudly, like the sound of a steam engine letting off pressure. It opened its mouth to reveal rows of obscene razor sharp teeth.

"Gim! Teeth! It's got teeth!"

"I know. Lots of them!"

"The Soft Worm doesn't have teeth. That's one of its primary characteristics. No teeth."

"Well, this thing's got bloody hundreds. I'm telling you, that book of your Dad's is useless."

Leah backed away from the creature, pulling Gim with her. "Unless that's not a Soft Worm. Unless it's something else altogether."

"Oh wonderful." The creature darted forward, then recoiled from Gim's burning flare. "Then what is it?"

"I don't think now is the best time to discuss research. I think now is an ideal time for us to get back to the surface. Whatever happens, just don't drop the bloody flare. It doesn't seem to like it. How many of those things have you got?"

"Two. Including this one. So what do we do?"

"We get out and then we pump this tunnel full of the most un-ecofriendly toxic pesticide-weedkiller I can get my hands on. Then we come back down, find the corpse and take samples."

The creature blinked at them and spun round, slithering down a fissure in the rock.

Silence.

"Where's it gone?" said Leah.

"Don't know."

"No, really, where has it really, actually gone?"

"Leah, it's gone. Gone is good, isn't it?"

"We need to know where this thing is."

"No! We need to get the hell away from this thing." Gim's flare sputtered.

"Timing. The secret to all good comedy." Leah pulled an

electric cell torch from her bag, just in case. She turned back the way they had come, but stopped short in sudden panic.

There were three tunnels. They had come down in the dark, and so had not noticed that there were three tunnel entrances to the large cavern. They had no way of knowing which was theirs. All lead upward at the same angle and all seemed to be as straight as each other.

"Which one? Leah, which one did we come down?"

"The one on the left. No, hang on it must have been the one on the right. No, it must have been..."

They looked at each other.

"We don't know, do we?"

"Split up?" Gim said, weakly.

"Good way to get eaten. On the plus side it doubles the chance of one of us getting back safely." Leah paused, straining her ears for the sounds of the beast. "Any ideas? Any at all?"

Gim strode forwards, confidently. "Middle one." he said.

"Why?" said Leah, running to catch him up.

"Toilet rule. Never fails."

"What toilet rule? What are you on about?"

"Three men's toilets at work, right?"

"If you say so."

"Right." They were walking fast now, panting at the exertion of striding uphill. "Three toilets. One nearest the door? Who goes in that one? I'll tell you; it's either the man who couldn't care what state the toilet is in and so picks the nearest one, or else it's the man who's got the shits and is running towards it undoing his trousers as he goes, hoping he makes it in time. Either way, you do not want to go there after them! Toilet three, furthest from the door: Who goes there? The man with something to hide, and that means he's either got something wrong with his guts and he's getting as far away from everyone else as he can out of human kindness, or else he's gone for a fiddle and is busy involved in some deviant sexual act. Either way, you don't want to go in there after him." They stopped dead, looking around them, half expecting the creature to reappear at any moment. "Where does that leave us? Toilet two, in the middle. The cleanest, most fragrant, most morally advisable toilet in the block."

The tunnel opened out into the large circular chamber they had first discovered just beyond the main shaft of the well. Gim turned to smile at her. "Never fails."

The ladder was still there.

"After you." said Gim, going first.

Leah smiled and gave a last look down the tunnel before starting up after him. Her foot missed a rung and she hung by her fingers, looking up.

The blood froze in her veins.

Above them. It was above them.

"Gim!" she hissed. "Stop! Look up!"

Gim looked up and saw that the wall of the tunnel was moving. There was something dark against the sky, something uncoiling itself and sliding down towards them. Leah dropped to the floor and backed away from the ladder, while Gim slowly climbed back down.

"Has it seen us?"

"Do you mean 'it' or 'they'? Who says there's only one of them?"

"I didn't think of that."

"Me neither."

They slowly backed away from the ladder towards the tunnel, trying to make as little noise as possible.

"Thing is," whispered Leah, close to Gim's ear, "it might be going out for the night again. It could be making its way up the tunnel, in which case we could still be all right. Let's wait a bit, see what happens."

Reaching into her bag, Leah found a small mirror. She held it up for Gim to see. "I'll have a peek round the corner. See if it's gone."

"Right. Why did you bring a mirror?"

"Because I'm a girl."

Leah slid forward and poked the mirror out from the tunnel, angled upwards so she could see the passage leading to the surface. It was hard to tell in the darkness, but she was fairly sure that the beast was still there. She could see it raising its head above the entrance to the well, looking this way and that, smelling the air with its tongue.

"I think it's going out. We'll give it a minute and then follow up." She patted Gim on the arm. "How are you doing? Apart from weeing in your pants, I mean."

"I think I've shat myself."

"Apart from that."

"Not very good. I just want to get out of here now."

The two them cautiously edged back towards the ladder; their eyes fixed on the open sky above them. There was no sign of the worm.

"Come on, let's do it before it comes back. Try and be as quiet as possible though, eh?" No sooner had Leah said the words, then there came the sound of shouting from above them. They recognised it at once. It was Krillan, barking orders to his militia.

"What the hell's he doing? It's the middle of the night!" hissed Leah.

"What the hell are we doing, it's the middle of the

night."

There was more shouting from above and the sound of a transport.

The two of them stayed where they were, frozen on the ladder.

"Do you think they've seen the worm?" said Gim, hopefully. "Perhaps they'll shoot it for us."

"Which would be good."

"But then they'll get the reward for finding it."

"Right now, that doesn't seem too much of a problem, I'd say."

They strained their ears again. It was hard to tell exactly what was going on, but they both clearly heard the words 'curfew' and 'looter'. Whatever Krillan and his men were up to, they weren't hunting the worm.

Frozen to the ladder, they heard the sounds of voices coming nearer. They both peered upwards, expecting to see the face of Krillan or one of his guards at any moment.

Two eyes appeared at the top of the well. Two bright green eyes. Gim shrieked and dropped to the floor.

It was the worm. The worm was slithering down towards them, no doubt moving away from Krillan and his men.

Leah jumped down to him.

"They've spooked it. Come on, move it!"

The two of them ran blindly now, trying not to hit their heads on the roof of the tunnel.

Behind them, in the dark, the worm cast a rueful eye upward at the sky above it, thwarted by the soldiers. But smelling their scent, it licked the walls and floor, and with a crafty, purposeful slither, it followed Leah and Gim down the tunnel.

CHAPTER SIX

The cavern at the top of the slope was dry, obviously above the level of the watercourse that usually fed the well.

"This is seriously bad," said Leah, feeding data from her wrist. "We're lost."

Gim rubbed his own wrist, puzzled. "How can that be?"

"We've travelled three miles straight since the last intersection. I think we've climbed the hill at the back of the village, only we've done it from the inside."

"That's weird."

"That's really weird."

"So we're probably near the Castle, then? So now what?"

"We think. Now then, weapons, we need weapons." Leah looked up at the ceiling of the chamber, thick with roots growing down, tendrils hanging in the empty air. "Think, think, think. What's on the hill? What grows on the hill leading up to the Castle, Gim? Can any of these roots be fashioned into something we can use?"

"Nothing."

"No. Never nothing, always something. There has to be something we can use as a weapon. What's up there?"

There came a noise from the far end of the tunnel.

"What makes you think we could use the plants as weapons? For all we know the worm might actually like them!" Gim said, eyeing the tunnel warily.

"I know! I knock you unconscious, shovel this stuff down your trousers and leave you for it." The noise grew louder. "Or we could just run away!"

They ran through the tunnels, conscious that any

moment a low ceiling could spell danger, and so they moved with one arm raised in front of them, expecting at any moment to hit the roof with their heads.

Turning a corner they noticed a faint greenish light, a phosphorescence.

"That's weird," said Gim, looking back anxiously. "Glowing roots."

Gim touched the roof. The roots hanging down had a faint green glow, which rubbed off on his fingers and sparkled. "What is this stuff? It smells like... like Meadowsweet. What smells like Meadowsweet, Leah?"

"It is Meadowsweet! Useful dried as bedding. Medicinal purposes include stemming bleeding, noted to be useful in warding off magical influences. Generally considered lucky. Do you actually know anything about plants, Gim?" Leah grabbed a handful of the roots and began rubbing them against her clothes. "Here, rub this stuff over you. It might help."

After they had covered themselves in Meadowsweet, the two friends ran on. Every now and then they caught the faint sound of slithering, of scales on rock, and knew that the beast was behind them. Leah began to get a nasty feeling that the creature was guiding them somehow, shepherding them on. After what seemed like ages, they found the walls of the tunnel becoming smoother, the rock more carefully hewn. In time it became brick until, finally, it opened up into a vast cavern. It reached up above them towards what looked like sky.

"Leah, it's daylight," said Gim. "Daylight. How long have we been down here?"

Leah looked up, astonished at the brightness, squinting after the dark of the tunnels.

"It's not daylight. Not unless there's something wrong with the sky. Look. The sky's generally blue, and that's...

well. Turquoise."

"Some sort of trick of the light? Does light do funny things if you look at it from the bottom of a cave?"

"Not unless you've been drinking."

"Wish I had been drinking," said Gim, sadly.

"Me too. What is it? What are we looking at here? It's the same colour as the Castle."

"Maybe it is the Castle."

Leah spun to face him. "Of course. We're beneath the Castle! We're looking up at it from deep underground. There must be a shaft from the Castle that leads straight down here. But why? Water supply?"

Gim suddenly grabbed his head, in pain. "Ow! Bloody eyes."

"You alright?"

"The Pixie. It's sending signals again. Must be nearby." Gim slammed his eyes shut against the pain, and the opened them again. "No. Gone, whatever it was." Gim looked at the walls of the cavern as they reached up towards the bright turquoise glow. "You think we could scale the walls?"

"If we had the right gear. Like a ladder..."

"Need a long one."

"... like a really long ladder. No. Funny, but I thought they'd have sensors down here. Charms, protective spells, that kind of thing. At the very least I thought they'd have some kind of fierce beast guarding the entrance." There came a sliding sound from behind them "Oh dear. You don't suppose that's what the worm is for do you?" The sound grew ever louder. "Run!" shouted Leah, pulling Gim behind her.

They ran across the large open area, as the sound of the beast grew louder still. They stopped in the middle of the cavern, lit by the glow from above. Frantically they looked about for a way out other than the one they had come in by. The noise from the entrance grew louder, but the beast did not enter the cavern. They could just make out its form in the darkness.

"What's it doing?" hissed Gim, holding onto Leah's arm.

"I don't know," whispered Leah. "It doesn't want to come into the cavern. Maybe it doesn't like the light, or something." Leah looked around her. "Or else it's scared of something else. What is down here right now?"

"Cave. Monster. Two people shitting themselves."

"There's nothing growing. No mould, no fungus, no lichen. There's nothing here at all. We're the only living things in this chamber."

"Great. Thanks. Really helps, that."

"So what I'm thinking is, why? Water, light, warmth, this place should be full of tiny little plants clinging to life, and yet there's nothing. Says to me that something stops life taking hold. Something keeps sterilising the area." She looked up. "Something like that!"

Above them a swirling shape was taking form. A complex series of patterns and spirals held together by magic as it wove the molecules in the air together into a swirling vortex of energy. "We need to get out here, Gim. Now!"

"But the Worm's still there. It's waiting."

Leah turned and looked at the shape in the tunnel.

"Clever little bugger. It knows. It knows what's going to happen and so it's pushed us this way." She paused, suddenly lost in thought. How clever was it exactly? The pressure of Gim's grip on her arm snapped her from her thoughts.

"Leah, think of something. Think of something now, because that thing above us can't be good. And I don't think we can scare it off by just rushing it and waving our arms."

Leah looked around her. "This place was built by people for a reason, and that means it will have an escape hatch."

"Unless the escape hatch was the tunnel we came in from. The one the worm is sitting in?"

Leah frowned. "Well, yes, there is that. But, no, it doesn't look right."

"What does look right then?" said Gim, taking off his backpack, ready to try and use it as a weapon if need be.

"I don't know. Something like –" Leah looked down, noticing the faint suggestion of a circle in the dust of the floor. "Something like this!" She dropped to her knees. "Help me Gim, there's a hatch."

"How did you know there would be a hatch?"

"It just makes sense that whoever built this thing, whatever it is, would put an escape hatch in place, just in case that," she gestured above her, "started to make it's way down when there were still people in here."

Ignoring the magical energy swirling above them, Leah took a closer look at the hatch. It was metal, with a large rusty hinge and handle, set into the floor. In the middle was a recess, the shape and size of a human hand. A nail size spike poked out where a wrist-port might connect. Without a second's hesitation, Leah plunged her hand into the recess, and felt the spike slide into her arm. The hatch began to ask her questions. Who she was, what she did, who she worked for. To her delight, and no small surprise, it seemed perfectly happy to know that she worked in the Gardens, and with a gentle orange glow, broke the seal around the edge. It raised itself a few inches and then stopped.

"It's jammed. The hinge is rusty, come on Gim, help me!" Together, the two friends pulled on the lid, but it still only budged a few more inches. Not enough to get either of them through. "Your bag!" shouted Leah, now feeling the warmth of the vortex descending on them. Snatching Gim's bag, she mashed the plants she had collected earlier into a pulp, before pulling out the bottle of cider she had seen Rendolph give him. Gim, to his credit, never complained as Leah poured the drink onto the pulped plant matter and mashed it onto the hinge, making a crude but hopefully effective lubricant. Again the two friends pulled, and this time the hinge obliged, just enough for two people to crawl through.

They were standing on a platform of some kind, the hatch above them. Without a word, the two of them grabbed the handle on the underside and pulled. In desperation they lifted their feet from the floor, hanging there and hoping that their combined weight would be enough to encourage the hatch to slam shut.

Around the edge of the hatch they could see the brightness getting more and more intense. The air became full of the scent of incense, of wood polish, of smoke and burnt leaves, and all the other aromas of magic, until with a gratifying KLAK the door slammed shut. They watched the hatch glow orange, red and then white as the heat of the magical energy filled the chamber. Then, as suddenly as it appeared, it receded, leaving the hatch glowing bright orange.

"Don't touch it Gim! It'll be hot for ages, yet."

"So what, we stand here in the pitch black until it cools down?"

"I don't know. Yes. Perhaps."

"What was that thing up there, Leah?"

"I don't know. Some kind of exhaust vent, perhaps?

Maybe there's so much magical-whatnots flying about the Castle that they need to vent it off from time to time? They're doing what everyone does with the rubbish; burn it and shove it underground and hope it goes away."

Leah suddenly felt her foot go cold.

"Whoa!" yelled Gim. "What was that?"

"Water. The chamber's flooding. Must be some kind of coolant running through from the chamber above. Maybe that's why the well ran dry in the village. Maybe the Castle is using too much. Whatever the reason, we need to get out of here."

"But you said we can't touch the hatch."

"No. Good point. Bugger."

They screamed as suddenly the platform they were standing on was pulled from beneath their feet, and the two of them plunged into water, their breath escaping as the freezing water compressed their chests.

They broke the surface, spluttering.

"Calm down! Calm down!" shrieked Leah, far from calm.

"Oh, that's cold!" yelled Gim. Thankful now for the faint phosphorescence of the Meadowsweet, as the two swam towards each other.

"See?" said Leah. "Good magic. We can find each other in the dark."

"Luck," said Gim, his teeth chattering.

"Same thing," said Leah. Something bumped against her. She recoiled in terror, until she realised it was her bag. "Come on, we should swim to the edge."

"Edge of what?" said Gim. "It might not have an edge. It might be miles across for all we know."

"Then why was there a metal platform above it? No this is man made. It's got an edge. And if there's an edge then there'll be a ladder."

"How do you know all this?" said Gim, trying to splutter out the words though the cold.

"Because it was built by intelligent people, and intelligent people tend to put ladders in places like this. Come on."

The two of them swam for three or four strokes before they came to a ledge that ran along the wall. As they made their way along, they found a series of iron hoops set into the wall. They began to climb, their clothes heavy and sodden. The ladder led them to another platform set up against the ceiling, and another door. As before, Leah thrust her hand into he recess. This time the door swung open at once. Above them was a smooth tunnel; the walls made entirely of a pale blue material, soft and warm to the touch.

"Leah, this is part of the Castle too, isn't it?"

"It looks like it. Yes. Come on."

Pulling the hatch closed behind them, the two friends made their way up the small passage. It was a relief to be out of the dark, and the pale aquamarine glow felt comforting after the nightmare of the dark tunnels. The air was sweet with the smell of lavender and honeysuckle, and the warm breeze that blew gently over them soon dried their wet clothes.

Eventually they came to a large blue room. There was a door at the far end but to their dismay it had no handle. They tried kicking it but it held fast. Their spirits sank, as they considered the possibility that they might have to retrace their steps and go back to the chamber filled with water.

"Now what?" said Gim, nervously eyeing the tunnel behind them. If the creature came upon them here, they would be done for.

"It's a door. It's lit up, there's breathable air; obviously people go through it. If we wait here long enough maybe someone will open it."

"And maybe they won't," said Gim.

"I know." Leah sat down, drawing her knees up to her chest. "We'll have to think of something else then."

"Like what?"

"I don't know yet."

Leah pulled out her father's book from the bag, and flicked through the pages once more. Whatever that thing, was, it wasn't a Soft Worm. But it was a worm of some kind. A great nasty one. Maybe it had things in common with other worms, some common weakness? "The Meadowsweet we passed earlier on. The worm didn't follow us through that section. I think it doesn't like it. Any idea why?"

Gim ran his fingers through his hair, his eyes still looking down the passage behind them. "Maybe someone put the Meadowsweet there to keep the worm away?" he said.

"Maybe" said Leah. "But maybe that means someone else knows the worm is here. Maybe someone put it here in the first place?"

"And maybe that means someone else knows we're here too?" said Gim.

High above them Niaal watched as a schematic of the tunnel systems beneath the Castle played across the dust hanging in the musty air of a seldom used chamber. Leah and Rendolph had done well to survive. Had they known of the true power of the worm they would not have dared to enter its lair. Niaal closed his eyes, communicating briefly with the creature, before he motioned with his hands in front of him, the image fading. He would let the worm toy with them for a while, before it fed.

Sliding his hands back under his bright yellow robes, Niaal turned and strode from the darkened room.

If the Castle had a heart, it was the chamber where the Mage Pillian lived. The holiest place in the land. The entrance was guarded day and night by soldiers dressed in blue ceremonial armour. The guard was changed every six hours, and it was considered one of the greatest honours in the land to serve there.

The door to Pillian's chamber was fifteen feet tall, and bound in the skin of a half dozen magical creatures, like the cover of some vast book. The entrance to the chamber was located in a large indoor courtyard, that opened upwards to a vast domed ceiling above. The enormous magical energies that were expended in the running of the Castle could not be seen or heard, but were rather felt. A constant pricking of the hairs on the back of the neck, a metallic tingling in the mouth.

The guards standing to attention exchanged worried glances as, without warning, the lights in the courtyard suddenly dimmed, and then burned again with their usual brilliance.

As they stood there, uncertain in their panic, the door opposite opened and a yellow clad Sage emerged, surrounded as always by his retinue of guards. The soldiers stiffened to attention.

"Halt in the name of the Mage!"

"Yes, yes, yes," said Niaal brusquely. "It's quite obviously me. Forget the protocol for a second, will you? What happened just then? What did you see?"

"The lights dimmed," said one solider, still at attention. "Just for a second, like, and then they went back on again."

"We were about to tell someone," said the other.

Niaal tutted. "No you weren't. You were going to carry on standing there like statues, because you didn't know what you should do." Niaal went up to the great door, and leaned his ear against it, like a man listening for a heartbeat. The two soldiers flicked the safety catch off their weapons and moved to stop him, but were held in check by two of the Chemical Warriors, who had guns trained on them before they could do much more.

"It's alright boys," said Niaal, still listening at the door. "Remember to play nicely." Pulling away Niaal drew a shape in the air, and the faces of four people, more Sages like Niaal, appeared in front him.

"What happened?" said Grefno, even before his image had stabilised. "What was that?"

"There was a fluctuation," said one of the Sages. "The magical conduits in the Castle suddenly seemed to constrict and then open again quickly. Like an artery in a human heart suddenly closing up."

"What does this mean?" said an elderly grey haired Sage. "Is the Mage aware?"

Niaal waved aside the image of the man. "I am outside his chamber now. Everything seems normal. There was a temporary dip in the lighting, but that is all. Distressing as this may be, I don't see that we have any major cause for concern."

No sooner had Niaal spoken the words, than the lights failed completely. The chamber was plunged into complete darkness, lit only by the ghostly apparitions of the Sages floating silently. Deciding they had seen quite enough, the two Castle guards dropped to immediate defence positions, their weapons raised in readiness.

Niaal's Chemical Warriors gazed at him with a worried expression. By the glow of the images they could see that he had gone white as a sheet, a heavy cold sweat on his brow.

"I think we have an emergency," he declared.

Gim and Leah were jolted by the sudden darkness.

"Whoa!" shouted Gim. "What's happening!"

"It's alright, it's alright," said Leah, clicking on a snap light. "The lights went out for some reason. They must have turned the power off, which could mean..." She pushed the door open. "Come on, before it comes back on again."

The two friends made their way through the narrow doorway, making sure to close it again behind them.

As they emerged into a large chamber, the lights suddenly came back on. Looking around they saw they were in the bottom of a large shaft that went up and up. At the top there was a silver sphere, no, not a sphere, an oval. More like a shiny metal egg, high above them.

"I have absolutely no idea where we are now," said Leah, open-mouthed. "I mean, we're in the Castle somewhere, but I don't know what this thing is or what it does."

As they walked around the chamber, they noticed another passage leading off in the opposite direction. Lacking any better plan, they set off along it. It made its way downwards, slowly and steadily. The blue walls gradually gave way until at last they faced a metal grill, large enough for them to squeeze through. From there onwards, the tunnel walls became stone and rock once more, the tunnel leading on and on, away from the

Castle.

Gim suddenly stiffened, clutching his head.

"Ow!" he cried. "That hurt."

"You smack your head?"

"No. I'm getting pictures again. I'm picking up signals. The Pixie must be near."

A smile came to Leah's face. "But they've only got a short range, you said so yourself. Which means..."

"Either it was carried off by something, or else we're somehow back near the tunnels where we first came in."

Heading on, Gim suddenly saw himself looking at himself and – disorientated by the experience – walked straight into a wall. Leah ran forwards to collect the tiny automaton, flicking the off switch before slipping it in her bag.

"We're near the well. We must be near the well. Look! This tunnel, I remember it."

"All look the same to me."

"No they don't. Come on."

Turning a corner they found, to their utter delight, that they were standing at the bottom of the well itself.

"Here, give me that brandy!" said Leah. Gim pulled it from his bag, took a swing and handed it to Leah As he did so, she was suddenly aware that there was something terribly wrong, something not right about his expression. His eyes were suddenly wide, pleading. He dropped to his knees.

Behind him the worm slid silently forward, it's tail raised high.

Leah now saw that it held a vicious barb, curved like a scorpion. It had struck Gim in the back. The creature flinched and the tail whipped towards her.

Lacking any form of defence she held her father's book in front of her face, screaming as she did so. The spike embedded itself in the thick hide of the tome, which it sought to remove by flicking its tail this way and that. Pages scattered. Leah hurled the flask of brandy at the beast, the glass shattering on impact. Picking up Gim's spare flare, she ignited it and bowled it at the creature's face.

The beast squealed in pain and shock at the flames that now covered its flesh, and suddenly it was gone. It was as if it had simply vanished...

"Gim? Gim? You still with me?"

"Ow."

Gim was lying on the floor, his face a deep purple bruise, but he was still alive.

Leah dragged him towards the ladder, putting him over her shoulder. She had no idea if she would be strong enough to carry him up but it was worth a try. Anything was better than staying down here. Slowly, one painful step at a time she did her best to climb with the unconscious man clutched to her. She knew it was not humanly possible to get him all the way to the top, but she had to try. Maybe she could wedge him part of the way up and leave him there while she ran for help. If the guards didn't shoot her first, that is.

Below her, she saw that her father's book burning. One page, caught in the updraught, landed on her arm. She caught sight of the illustration on the paper. It showed the exact same creature they had just seen. In the woodcarving it was resting on a pile of corpses, its tongue licking the empty eye sockets of a human skull.

'Gentle Worm. This creature hath a venomous bile. It hath a spike which woundeth but kills not. To kill the creature you must...'

"Ow! I'm on fire! It's burning me!" cried Gim, suddenly conscious again.

Leah shouted out "No! Stay still!" But it was too late. The page fell back down into the darkness below.

"What did you do that for?"

"Because my sodding leg's on fire!" Gim swung his arms round and grabbed the ladder, rubbing his legs together to put out the flame.

"You alright?" Leah said, grateful beyond imaging that he was now taking his own weight again.

"Not really. I've been stung by a giant snake-thing and my leg was on fire."

"Can you make it up the ladder?"

"I don't know. Everything's gone a bit woozy. What happened to me? I though I was dead."

"I don't know. But we really do have to get you out of here. Come on, keep climbing. We'll do it together. I won't leave you here, I promise."

Slowly, painfully, the two of them pulled their way up the ladder, while the fire below them fizzled and went out. Leah tried not to think of how fast the worm had moved, and how quickly it would be able to follow them up. But of the creature there was no sign.

She cursed herself for a fool for taking the book into tunnel without making a copy of the relevant sections first.

The last ten feet of the ladder seemed to Leah as if it may as well have been a thousand, but somehow they managed to get there. But just as Leah had one hand on the outside of well, there came a scurrying, a wet slapping sound below them.

"No!" she shrieked. It was the worm again, making its way up after them. Leah dragged Gim, whose eyes were now lolling, his face an unhealthy hue. "Come on!" She shouted. The worm was coming and then –

– and then suddenly there were more pairs of arms,

hauling the two of them up, dragging them over the lip
of the well.

CHAPTER SEVEN

Sergeant Wallas looked at Leah, his face full of confusion.

"Leah? What the in the nine hells were you doing in the well?"

"Quickly, there's something coming! Get away!" shouted Leah, wide eyed in fear trying to drag the now unconscious Gim away from the well. She was surrounded by soldiers. There was no sign of Rendolph.

"Whoa, steady now. What're you talking about? What's going on, Leah?"

"Get away. It's in there, some creature. A giant worm!"

Wallas was puzzled, but swung his blaster from his shoulder anyway, thumbing the safety catch.

"A worm? A worm in the well?" He signalled to his men who shouldered their rifles warily. Wallas unclipped a flare from his webbing, and lobbed it into the hole. He counted to three and then thrust himself forward to peer over the lip. As his eyes adjusted to the darkness he saw something move, far below him.

"Keep back!" shouted Leah.

Lights filled the square as a military transport pulled up. Captain Rilston and a squad of Castle guards jumped down, guns at the ready, their blue uniforms spotless in the torchlight.

"Caught one, have we?" Rilston strode across the square, hands behind his back. "And it's Miss Carleaf, what a pleasant surprise. Out for a stroll, were we? And who's this with you? Oh, one of your little friends. Fast asleep I note. Dear me, you really must learn to hold your drink better."

Wallas stepped back from the well, resetting the safety catch on his weapon.

"Tell him, Wallas. Tell him what's down there." Leah said.

Wallas stood awkwardly to attention.

"I'm not sure, Miss. I mean, I saw something, I think. Couldn't say what."

Leah left Gim lying on the ground and rushed to the well mouth. "Captain, there's a worm down there, a giant beast. It attacked my friend."

Rilston walked over to the well and peered down. "In the well? You mean you were down there? Whatever for?"

"We were looking for it."

Rilston snorted. "I wasn't aware you'd lost one, Miss Carleaf." He turned to Wallas. "Have these two taken to the militia barracks for further questioning. No idea what they're up to, but the curfew is to be strictly enforced. If I don't have a reasonable answer to what I believe to be a set of reasonable questions, I'll have the pair of them taken to the Castle for interrogation if need be. That is all, Sergeant."

Wallas walked over to Leah, slinging his rifle over his shoulder. "You heard him, Miss."

Leah knelt beside Gim, cradling his head. She looked up at Wallas, sharply. "This man is hurt, Sergeant. He may well be dying. He needs immediate attention."

"Not for me to say, Miss."

"Not for you to –? Sergeant, his face is bright purple! Look at him! He was stung by the worm and I'd say he needs urgent medical attention. Please, get him into a transport and take him to the hospital. It's on the way to the barracks."

Wallas hesitated

"Look. If he dies on us, then I promise I'll let you shoot him if that it will make you feel any better!"

Gim was taken into the isolation ward on an army stretcher, carried by two militiamen wearing gas masks, just in case. Guards were posted on the ward, although it was obvious to everyone that Gim was in no state to escape. A drip was inserted into his right arm, while his wrist-port was attached to a bedside computer that monitored his vital signs. Although satisfied that he did not show symptoms of the sickness, they decided to take no chances.

Leah sat on the single plastic chair in her cell and stared at the door. Rilston's men had brought her to the barracks, after she too had been tested for the sickness. It was a blockhouse, designed to house about twenty soldiers, with a high perimeter wall, a couple of cells and a central control room

A guard brought her a warm drink and something to eat. He was young and obviously uncomfortable to be her jailor.

"Any further news of my friend Gim?" said Leah, sipping the drink.

"None that I know of. Has he got the sickness?"

"What? No he hasn't. He was stung by the worm! However it is that people are getting ill, it's not because they were stung by enormous monsters. You need to tell your Captain that there's a creature in the well, and that it's got to be taken care of."

"I'll do what I can, Miss. But I was only told to bring you something to eat and drink before they get round to questioning you." Leah looked at her food, suddenly suspicious. The boy laughed. "It's alright, Miss, I haven't put anything funny in it. It's just food, really it is."

Leah took a mouthful and cried.

Grefno strode along the passageway between the War Room and the Council Chamber, his warriors struggling to remain a dignified distance behind him. In the past few days he had developed an unseemly gait that had caused less generous souls to whisper behind his back that he was damaging the dignity of his calling. Grefno knew, and didn't particularly care. He had been stuck in his books for three days now, trying to understand the sickness and what might have caused it. He knew he should be gearing his thoughts towards the impending war, but the more he tried to steer his thoughts in that direction, the more unfocussed and distracted he became. It was only by concentrating on the sickness that he felt truly engaged.

Deciding to allow his thoughts free rein, he had walked away from the war altogether and was now wholly concentrating on finding the cause of the disease.

There were so many variables to consider. The illness didn't seem to be as random in its choice of victims as Grefno had at first thought. The loss of the Gardeners was a worry, but over the last few days he had seen soldiers struck down and local civil servants, while it seemed to ignore the lower classes as often as not.

Grefno had considered diet, lifestyle, all the factors he could in his quest for a cure, for if a solution could be found, then there would be no need for war. And war was something to be avoided at all costs.

As a young man Grefno had served in the front line overseas. Distant allies had been threatened, and they had gone to their aid. As a Chemical Warrior he had been assigned to a logistics unit, supposedly supporting front line troops, but in a career destroying tactical blunder, a senior general had allowed the line to be over run, meaning Grefno was caught behind enemy lines. He had formed a loose group of soldiers, engineers and stores clerks, and together they had fought their way back home against incredible odds, and in the most inhospitable of terrain.

Sages did not suffer nightmares. Their dreams were far more lucid and valuable than that. The other men in his unit were not so fortunate, and were still plagued by horrors on nights when the air was warm and the air thick with pollen. They had been in a jungle, knee deep in water for weeks, with constant rain and stifling heat. Apart from the enemy, who seemed perfectly at ease in such hostile terrain, there were other threats. Trees that swallowed men whole, leeches the size of bricks and lights that would lure a man off into the swamp.

Grefno reached the lobby, and strode out into the cool marble entrance. Four men waited for him, one in grey, two in the black armour of serving infantry. At their head stood General Vale. Without a word, Grefno gestured them towards him, and together they filed into a brass elevator cage. As it ascended, Grefno at last spoke.

"My esteemed colleague, the Sage Niaal, says that war is inevitable," he said. The General coughed, flicking a glance at his comrades. Like him, they were white haired and getting on in years, though still commanding in appearance.

"War is seldom inevitable, Grefno. It may be that a certain amount of sabre rattling along the borders will be enough, or it may be that we need to project sufficient power into disputed territories to convince them of our resolve."

A short man in a grey naval uniform cut in, saying, "There are no disputed territories. What we are talking about is stealing several hundred miles of someone else's land. There is no dispute. It's downright hostility. We would be outraged if this were done to us by another state."

Grefno led them out of the elevator and into a chamber that was open to the sky. A Thought Ship wavered in the breeze above them. This was the Mage's personal hanger. Grefno clicked his fingers and a faint blue powder fell around them, forming a bubble with them inside.

Grefno faced them. "There. Now no one can hear us. Even in the Castle we must be careful." He folded his hands beneath his robes, projecting an air of calm, as he described the situation and the lack of a cure for the sickness, with all that entailed. "To that end it has been suggested that we annexe land from Prash-Romaria. It will be a brief, bloody conflict which we expect to win. Our nation will survive." He looked around at them, appalled by his own words. "The Sages suggest that we save ourselves by murdering our own countrymen, and by openly stealing from our neighbours."

The naval officer adjusted his collar. "It's madness. Surely we can do better than this? What if we go to them in the spirit of friendship and ask for help?"

"That has been tried. Diplomats report that the Prash-Romarians are at best unwilling to help, at worst may consider destroying all of Allesh by fire themselves, in order to contain the sickness. Already we have seen troop movements on their borders."

"Well, we cannot expect them to sit idly by as we move our troops nearer to their territory," said the Admiral. "I know we wouldn't stand for it, were our situations reversed."

"If we attack then the conflict will escalate in no time at all." General Vale said. "The Prash-Romarians are fierce warriors, and are ably supported by cunning wizards. Tanks and shells would quickly churn up any farmland we might hope to gain. We would take hundreds of miles of arable farmland and quickly turn them into a muddy swamp filled with trenches and dead bodies. We could be no better off."

"Yes," said Grefno, simply. "Quite possibly. But if we do nothing, then we will almost certainly die, unless a cure is found, and found quickly." They stood in silence, the fate of the country sat on their shoulders.

"The Mage," said General Vale. "What does the Mage say?"

"He is not to be disturbed. He is in deep meditation and must not be contacted under any circumstances."

"But surely," spluttered the navy officer. "Surely a situation like this is so exceptional that protocol can be side-stepped?"

Grefno avoided his gaze. "Under any circumstance. Sorry my friends, but we have to deal with this by ourselves."

"But this is ridiculous! What's the point of having a Mage, what's the point in all this," Vale gestured around them at the Castle, "if the Mage refuses to even talk to us? Duty is one thing. But it cannot and must not make us blind to reason!"

Grefno held his hands together in front of him in a gesture of humble supplication. "I know you are right.

And that makes it all the worse. We must find a way around this, before war becomes the only option open to us."

The two men glared at each other, before the General placed a conciliatory hand on Grefno's shoulder.

"We will find a way round this. We always have. Together."

The bubble burst around them, and they were back in real-time again.

The General flexed his shoulders, feeling the stiffness of the years suddenly in his bones. "Come my friends, we must address the Sages."

"I will not be joining you," said Grefno. "For now I am needed elsewhere. If a cure can be found, then I must do all I can to find it. If we fight the sickness, then perhaps we will have no need to fight our neighbours."

Back in his study, Grefno poured over figures and calculations, the numbers blurring in his head like fireballs swung by dancers at harvest time. His wrist-port was linked to the Castle mainframe, feeding him a constant stream of information. Grefno was pushing himself beyond all reasonable tolerances now, and was closer to breaking than he would ever admit.

Every time he thought he saw a solution, it vanished, every time he thought he had turned a corner it led only to another dead end.

The sickness was so hard to pinpoint, to hold down for a second.

He sat in his favourite chair, looking blankly at the numbers hanging in the air before him.

As a boy he had gone fishing with his father. They had

meant to catch saltfish, but he had caught an eel instead. He remembered how they had tried to hold it to take the hook from its mouth, and how it had slithered and slid across the small boat, scaring him. Every time his father grabbed it, it would slide through his fingers. Grefno had not liked even small garden earthworms as a boy, and to him the eel seemed like some horrible worm, only the length of his arm.

Grefno sat very still and gently massaged his wrist. He was being told something. His mind was telling him something, but what was it? Something about fathers, something about... fishing?

His fingers flicking, he sent out a broad media scan to the news channels. News agencies in other countries were complaining about fluctuations in the magical energies that sustained them. There had been talk for several weeks now of the possibility that the magical energy that flowed across the world of Inan was somehow being interfered with. The Mages of Inan were apparently unaffected. Nonetheless, he was reassured that other wizards in other states were looking into it, as the problem seemed to be global in nature. It couldn't fall to a small country the size of Allesh to solve the world's problems, after all.

Closer to home there were the usual reports of people dying, the aftermath of the fire in the Gardens, news along the borders, patrols ambushed. He looked again at the reports of the sickness in the Garden. The Gardeners all dead; the Gardens now being run by soldiers, the only survivors of the original work-force being a girl and two local boys.

The girl had now been arrested. Her name was Leah Carleaf.

Carleaf? He focussed on her story, suddenly alert. The daughter of Griggo Carleaf? Now there was a thing.

She had been arrested, with a young man, for breaking curfew. Well, that seemed obvious enough; young people wanting privacy under cover of darkness was nothing new. What he heard next made him sit bolt upright in his chair, his heart racing.

She was claiming that she had seen a giant worm.

The image of his father with the eel ran through his mind once more.

There were no giant worms in this part of Inan. Not even in zoos. Grefno checked Leah's story again.

Pulling himself free from the cables and plugs that attached him to his work, Grefno got up and made his way to the door. He must speak with this girl at once. His guards were waiting for him outside, vigilant as ever. "Come," he said and they followed. It was a matter of minutes before Grefno was in the town and outside the barracks, the brown-uniformed militiamen snapping to attention as he came forwards. The duty officer was there to greet them, as soon as they were inside the main compound.

"Honoured Sage, you grace us," he muttered, unsure of protocol. "To what do we owe the pleasure?"

"The girl," snapped Grefno. "I need to see her."

"Of course. Please, follow me." The officer led them along a brightly lit corridor, to a wooden door held in place with heavy iron bolts. A latticework of delicate red laser light flickered across it, picking out the dust motes that hung heavy in the air.

Leah was lying on her bed when the door swung open, and two bright yellow clad Chemical Warriors entered the cell. She recognised one as the man who had given her sedatives on that first morning, the day her friends in the Garden had been killed. If he recognised her, then his eyes betrayed nothing. Grefno entered. He looked her up and down. "Leah Carleaf? I believe we have much to discuss."

Inside the cell, Grefno sat on the bed next to Leah. Leah, unsure as to what was happening, sat unmoving watching him and the guards. Eventually he spoke. "You have seen a worm." It was a statement, not a question.

"Yes. Last night. It's in the well in the market square."

"Why do you think there is a worm in the well?"

"Because I saw it. Because I climbed down into the well and saw it for myself."

"Why did you climb down into the well?"

"To look for the worm."

"Why did you think there was a worm in the well?"

Leah looked at him, not sure if he was an idiot or playing games. "Because I saw the worm in a magical note left by the old Head Gardener. He had seen it in the market place, and I took it to be a Soft Worm. I read in one of my father's books that Soft Worms are prized by Wizards. I thought if we caught it then we might earn the gratitude of the Mage and he would help my mother."

"Why did you not tell the local militia captain?"

"Because he's a prick?"

"He is. But he also has the power to send men down there and search for it. Instead we find your friend Gim gravely injured in hospital, and you locked up in a holding cell. So I ask again, why did you not tell the Captain?"

Leah burst into tears. Grefno shot a glance at his warriors, one of whom handed Leah a blue phial.

With a quick movement she smacked the ampoule from his hand.

"No! Bloody stuff's messed me around enough as it is!"

she shouted. Her sudden outburst bringing her quickly back to her senses.

"Leah, it's alright," said Grefno. "You've been under a great deal of pressure recently. It's perfectly understandable. Added to this the fact that, despite your junior position, you now find yourself running the Gardens must be a lot to take on board. All you have to work with are local soldiers who don't know the first thing about horticulture." He smiled. "How am I doing?"

Leah looked at the man anew. "That's about it. That and the fact that I've got myself locked in jail after spending half the night being chased through tunnels by a sodding great big monster, which might have killed one of my friends."

"Describe the creature to me," said Grefno, his fingers drawing patterns in the air as he did so.

"It was about thirty feet long," she said. As Leah described the creature, it took shape in the air in front of her, Grefno using his power to conjure up a picture of it. "It had scales and horrid eyes."

"How did it attack you?" asked Grefno, quietly.

"It stung my friend with a spike in its tail. And it had teeth. Lots of them."

"Soft Worms have no teeth, Miss Carleaf."

"I know that. I think it's something else. I can't be sure, but I think it's a Gentle Worm." Leah watched the colour drain from Grefno's face. "You know what one is then?"

Grefno flicked his fingers and the shape blurred, and reasserted itself as the same beast Leah had seen in the well. "Is this the beast you saw in the well?"

"No mistaking it. Not the sort of thing you'd forget in a hurry."

"Miss Carleaf, you need to be absolutely and completely certain of this, because if you are wrong, then what I am about to do will get us all into a great deal of trouble."

"I'm sure," said Leah. "This is the thing we saw last night. Gentle Worm. Right there."

"The Gentle Worm is poisonous, Miss Carleaf. It delivers a complex poison through its bite. It also has a less-venomous sting on its tail, which is fearsome enough on its own." Grefno gazed at the image, slowly shaking his head. "But the very worst thing about a Gentle Worm is that it is covered in a toxic coating of venomous slime, which renders it utterly inedible. The creature is a savage and ferocious predator, which cannot be eaten by any other creature on the planet."

"But if it's in the well," said Leah. "then it's been in the water supply."

"Yes. I believe we have found the source of the illness, at least. The toxic slime given off by the beast must have found its way into the water supply."

"The Head Gardener. He changed the irrigation routes to the garden. He saw the worm himself. I know because he left a message." Leah felt hope surge within her. "So if you can find this beast and capture it, then can you create an antidote?"

"If we find the beast, yes. I can create a serum that undoes the damage caused by drinking water contaminated by the worm."

"But how did it get here?" said Leah, all fear now gone, as she found herself wrapped up in the mystery. "If they don't live here, then how did it get here?"

"I think it is being used as a weapon, Leah. There are all kinds of warfare," he said, counting them off on his fingers. "Psychological, conventional, nuclear, biological, magical, botanical," and here he turned to face her, "And zoological."

"But why now?"

"I don't know. But this worm is not a native of these parts. My guess is someone placed it here for a reason."

"If you say so. But again, why now?"

Grefno sighed. "Leah, there was a fluctuation in the magical fields surrounding the Castle last night. The magical energy that sustains us, emanating from the Mage, stopped. For a whole thirty seconds. That may not seem long to you, but had we been in a state of war, then it would have been enough of a window to allow for our total destruction through magical means, had our enemies noticed it. And there are one or two still bearing huge grudges from the last war. Tell me, is there anyone here you can trust? Anyone in the barracks?"

"What do you mean?"

"I mean what I say. I need you alive, Miss Carleaf. Is there anyone here you can trust with your life in my absence?"

"Yes. Wallas. Old guy out front? He was a friend of my father."

"I know Wallas very well. And you are right to trust him. If at all possible, don't let him out of your sight, and make sure he has his gun with him at all times. He is an excellent shot. Follow any instruction he gives you, to the letter."

"Why? You think someone will come after me?"

Grefno paused. "Miss Carleaf, unless I am mistaken, we are all being played for fools in some far deadlier game than worm hunting. I will send help as soon as I can. I am off to tell news of your worm to General Vale, who is quite possibly the only man in the country right now with the power to stop this madness that we seem determined to march straight into. Should anything happen to me, you will need to go to General Vale yourself."

"What? Sorry, I work in the Gardens, how the hell am I

supposed to bend the ear of a general?"

"He may not listen to you, but he will listen to Wallas. Talk to no one, trust no one, except Wallas."

"Why is he so important? Wallas, I mean?" asked Leah, suddenly suspicious. "Why should I trust him just on you word?"

"I fought alongside Sergeant Wallas long ago," said Grefno. "He was a good soldier. As was your father. I shall be back soon as I can, Leah."

With that Grefno was gone. Leah slumped on her bed, suddenly tired, wishing that she could sleep.

Sergeant Wallas stiffened to attention as Grefno and his men came down the corridor towards him.

"Please Wallas, you do not need to salute me," said Grefno, placing a hand on the old soldier's shoulder. "We have been through too much for that."

"It's not the person, but the office," said Wallas, simply.

"And you are worth far more than the office, my friend. I owe everything to you. You know this."

"Begging your pardon, but Miss Carleaf? Leah, I mean. What's going on? She was in the well, breaking curfew, and going on about worms. I mean, we all like a drink now and then, but the middle of a curfew isn't the best time. Especially with the sickness and all."

"Miss Carleaf has seen something extraordinary and is, as a result, a key witness to solving the mystery of the sickness. If I am right then her life may be in real danger. As things stand, a cell may yet be the safest place for her. However, if things get complicated, I will need you to protect her. Do you understand me, Sergeant?"

"As always, Sir."

"Good. I need to go to the Castle and organize our affairs. As soon as I'm sure it's safe, I want Leah Carleaf brought up to the Castle. We also have to switch off the water supply to the village and the Castle at once. Whatever else happens, don't let anyone drink the water. We need to tell the villagers that the illness is being transmitted by a complex poison in the water."

The two old friends nodded to each other, and then Grefno was gone, his retinue scouring for signs of danger as always.

"How do you know him then?" said a young officer, pointing to Grefno.

"Battle of Misbone Creek. Two hundred of us went into the swamp. Three of us came out. We had to carry Grefno, mind. He'd fried his brains on stimulants trying to find a safe path." Wallas felt the old wounds ache as the memory returned. "It was the plants, you see? Botanical weapons stuffed full of magic. Crack a man's limbs and suck the marrow straight out. Dreadful thing to see. Now, I'm standing here and not moving from outside this cell, so why don't you run along and get me a bite to eat, lad?"

With a shrug, the young soldier went off to the kitchen, hoping that one day he'd have stories of his own to bore younger men with.

In the kitchen, he washed his hands in the regulation manner and began to put together a plate of cold food from the store. Some cheese, some bread, and some herbs. It was while he was running these under the tap that he caught sight of something moving through the thick window. The windows were arrow-slit thin and made of a glass would take the impact a mortar shell without breaking. The soldier looked again, wondering why, if someone were mooching around outside, it didn't set the sensors off.

Picking up the tray of food, he went out into the corridor, and instead of going back to where Wallas was guarding the cell, he turned instead towards the guardroom.

It was empty.

"Where is everybody?" he called. "Someone outside? Come on boys, Wallas will have your nuts for marbles if he catches you away from the post. What's going on?" At the door to the courtyard, his eyes strayed to the communications panel on the wall by the door. It was mangled, wires hanging out. He was still looking at the comms unit a split second later when the door opened and the beast sprang forwards.

Screaming, he lifted the tray in front of him, fending off the creature as it lunged for him. Scrabbling backwards he hurried out the guardroom, the worm in pursuit.

"Wallas!" he shrieked, "Help!"

In desperation the officer hit the fire alarm. At once sprinklers opened up. The soldier ran down the corridor, the creature slithering after him. As he turned the corner, he ran straight into Wallas, unclipping his gun at the sound of the commotion.

"It's behind me!" he shouted.

"Drop!" shouted Wallas.

The soldier hit the floor as Wallas took aim, but there was nothing there. The corridor behind the soldier was empty.

"What happened?" shouted Wallas, his gun darting from side to side as he tried to find a target.

"Worm, Sergeant! Monster, it is. It looks like it's killed the others."

"Where was it? This creature?"

"It was outside in the courtyard. It must have got the

lads when they went outside for a smoke."

Wallas stayed motionless, his finger on the trigger, knuckles white.

"Now, I'm going to stay here and shoot the arse off anything that comes round the corner. I suggest you go and get Miss Carleaf out of the cell and get her to safety. The Sage who was here told me to keep her alive, and leaving her alone with creatures that have just wiped out my boys doesn't seem to follow that to the letter."

The soldier backed towards the cell. "Miss? We need to get you out of here." He said, entering the cell.

Leah was cowering in a corner, worried by the shouting from outside.

"Why? What are you going to do?"

Sergeant Wallas' voice came from down the corridor. "It's alright, Leah, do as Private Shaule says. We've got ourselves a problem and I need to get you away from here to somewhere safer."

"I'm in a prison cell that's probably been designed to withstand an air strike! I thought that was safe enough?"

"Tell her what you saw, Shaule."

Leah turned to the solider. "What? What's happening?"

"Great big worm? About thirty feet long, ugly bastard. Lots of teeth, pointy tail."

Following the soldier out into the corridor, Leah reached over to the wall and detached a fire extinguisher. The soldier looked at her, quizzically.

"Better than nothing," she said.

Wallas appeared down the corridor, his handgun replaced with an impulse rifle, something more substantial and packing more firepower. He had another weapon slung over his shoulder, which he handed to Shaule. "I suggest we run for it," he said. "As soon as I open the main door, we run forward. I'll release a volley to the left, you spray the right, Shaule. Leah, you keep in the middle. Whatever happens to anyone else, you keep running. On my mark. One, two, three!" The door hissed open and the three figures sprinted through into the guardroom, Wallas and Shaule letting loose bursts of impulse fire. Still running they hurtled through the now open door to the courtyard.

There was nothing there. Wallas kept his weapon pressed to his shoulder, scouring the rooftops and the perimeter fence. "Right, here's the plan. You take Miss Carleaf here, and make for the village. Try and get her to somewhere safe. The inn's usually a safe bet. I'm going to try and get to the Castle to raise the alarm."

"The Sage, Grefno? He said I was supposed to stick to you like glue. I really think we should stick together," said Leah. "Like glue."

"So do I, Miss. But we need to keep you safe, and we need to get help from the Castle. I think taking you with me is too risky, and so the safest thing is for the two of you to try and find what refuge you can in the village. I think this thing was sent to kill you. I think you saw something when you were in the well. Something that they didn't want you to see, whoever they are. Now go. Go now, Leah."

With a nod to Wallas, Leah and Shaule ran off towards the village, eyeing every tree and bush as they went for signs of trouble. Wallas covered them with his impulse rifle until they were out of sight, and then set off towards the Castle.

Wallas' thumb brushed the safety catch on his weapon. He knew he was capable of killing another man, so a beast would be easy, if only he could get it in his sights.

At the junction with the main road Wallas stopped to get his breath back and work out some kind of plan. Leah and Shaule should be able to reach the Inn easily enough, and would hopefully raise the alarm from there.

The outer perimeter wall of the Castle had a gatehouse. It was surrounded by powerful spells, and bristled with arcane energy. As he ran towards it, Wallas felt the hairs on his arms and neck prickle, as they began to rise. Deciding it would be a bad time to be mistaken by the sentries for an armed madman and shot, he slung his weapon over his shoulder and slowed down to a fast walk. A hundred yards from the gatehouse he began to get cross with the guards on duty for not challenging him. At fifty yards he was mentally composing the dressing down he would give them when he confronted them. At ten yards, he realised that something was very wrong and unslung the weapon from his shoulder, his finger covering the trigger.

"Guardroom!" He called out. "Guardroom to the gate! Friend approaching."

There was no reply. Again he called out. "I say again, friend approaching!"

Nothing.

Wallas advanced slowly, viewing everything through the sights of the weapon.

He entered the guardroom looking for signs of trouble. It was inconceivable to his mind that the worm had reached the outer wall of the Castle without being seen, but all the same it paid to be wary.

A magical picture hung in mid-air, showing the Castle layout. He brushed it aside and opened up a new channel.

A blue uniformed Castle guard swam into view. He looked at Wallas with some surprise.

"Castle Control. Go ahead, Gate Nine?"

"Castle Control, this is Sergeant Wallas. The post is deserted, repeat. I am armed and holding the position, awaiting further instructions, over."

"You're saying they've deserted their post, Sergeant?"

"Saying nothing of the sort. But whatever's going on, they're not here." Wallas stopped, suddenly alert to the sound of movement from outside. "Didn't you think it strange that you hadn't heard from them recently? It's been a while since I had to pull guard duty, but we had to check in every twenty minutes back in my day."

"The comms have been on and off all day. One minute they're up, the next they're down. No idea what's happening. We've got people looking at it now. I'm sending a squad down now, sergeant, they'll be with you in five minutes."

"Advise you cancel that order. Whatever this is about, it could be that they're trying to get you to open the main gate. Given what's happened here I'd say that wasn't a good idea."

"... Are you asking for quarantine?"

Wallas edged towards the door, never taking his eyes from his sights.

"Repeat, are you requesting quarantine? Sergeant, is there any sign of the guardroom detail? Any sign at all?"

"Nothing. They've just gone." Wallas slowly edged away from the screen, his eyes on the door, the weapon pressed firmly into his shoulder. "What's your name, soldier?"

"Mykaze."

"Right then, Mykaze, here's what we're going to do. You're going to contact your duty officer at once, and tell him that we have a dangerous beast outside the Castle wall. Under no circumstances are you to let anyone in or out until we're sure the coast is clear."

"Done," said the soldier, manipulating data buds floating in front of him.

"Secondly," said Wallas, "I need a message carried through to one of the Sages. Yes, I know it's unorthodox, but believe me he'll want to be informed. Contact the Sage Grefno, and tell him that Sergeant Wallas would like a word, urgent like."

"Really? What, I just send that message off, and he'll get back to me?" He laughed. "Sages don't do that."

"This one will. You need to send it on code Auburn 72. Just that. Sent to the office of the Sage Grefno."

Putting the gun to his shoulder Wallas edged his way around the door, fearing the worst. The worm had killed the men in the gatehouse, of that much he was certain. But how had it just vanished again? Furthermore, why had it not attacked him? And if he was safe, for the moment at least, did that mean that Leah was now in trouble?

Wallas backed slowly into the room, pulled up a chair facing the door and waited.

CHAPTER EIGHT

"You want us to do what?" The Mayor stood in front of Leah, his face white and hands balled into fists on his hips.

"I said that we need to arm ourselves. We need to find this beast and either kill it, or else capture it until it can be transported away from here safely."

"And why in the fifty-nine buggering hells would we want to do that? Why would we want to go out there and do a thing like that?"

The meeting was not going entirely as well as Leah had hoped, all things considered. On making her way to the village, she had ran to the market square and had rung the alarm bell, used only in times of national distress and for the occasional emergency wedding. One by one, people had opened windows and peered out warily. One or two had armed themselves, fearing the worst.

During the war, there had been established protocols for use in an emergency, and many of those who had been air raid wardens or civil defence volunteers found themselves falling back into well rehearsed routines at the sound of the alarm. The children of the town were gathered together and led away to the village shelter, a large underground bunker with a heavy iron door. One or two others began digging out their old equipment for use in emergencies. Axes, shovels and blankets were found and carried outside, although many preferred to wait in their own homes until they knew for certain what was going on.

Calling from street to street, Leah and Shaule had summoned a large crowd of villagers to the Inn.

"Look, I'll try again," Leah said. "There's this thing in

the well. It's a sort of worm, a great big monster. It's called a Gentle Worm, and it shouldn't be here."

"Bloody right it shouldn't be here," muttered a red-faced farmer. "Who brought it here anyway? Was it you?"

"What? No it wasn't!" She blustered, trying to make them see sense. "Look, the worm is almost certainly the cause of the sickness, according to one of the Sages. I mean, it's a bit too much of a coincidence isn't it? Sodding great beast roaming the streets while we all go down with a mystery illness? Which reminds me! Don't drink the water. It's poisoned. Best if you stick to bottled drinks."

A small woman in glasses held up her hand. "Excuse me? Why don't the militia take care of it? Isn't that what they do? We have enough of them in the barracks, after all. Why don't we get them to go and shoot it?"

Leah looked over at Private Shaule. "Everyone at the barracks is dead. All of them. The worm killed them. I made it here to warn you. Captain Krillan, wherever he is, will hopefully be here as soon as Sergeant Wallas can get word to him. In the meantime we arm ourselves, barricade the village and hold the thing off until the army get here. If we put people on the rooftops, and block the roads, shutter all windows we can turn the town square into a fortress."

"Of course, there is always the chance that this thing is just after you, Miss Carleaf," the small woman said. "I mean, if it's following your scent, then you could always go somewhere else."

"What makes you think it wants me?"

"Well, you saw it in the well, you say? And then it seems to have followed you to the barracks? So why shouldn't it follow you here? Nothing personal, but perhaps you should go. For the good of everyone."

One or two of the larger men looked at each other, as if trying to read what the other was thinking. Leah was tall and young, but it wouldn't be too difficult to overpower her.

Private Shaule flicked the safety catch off his weapon. It made a loud enough click to let everyone know this was not a viable option.

"Thank you, Shaule. Well, I think that answers that one." Leah said. "Any further suggestions. Sensible ones?" The people in the Inn looked at each other. The small woman shrugged her shoulders; she evidently thought her idea a good one.

"Right then," Shaule said. "Here's what we'll do. I'll set up a defensive position at one end of the high street, which will allow me to cover all points leading from the barracks to the village. I need volunteers to stake out the well. If that's where the creature is heading, then we might be able to intercept it on the way through, should it manage to get past my blockade. I don't know what weapons you've got here, but I know there's enough poaching going on to mean that at least some of you have something that may bring the creature down. You don't need to be great shots, just don't panic and start blasting off wildly. The creature is fairly large, so if you take your time and choose your target carefully you should be able to get at least one shot off before..." He paused. "Well, if enough of you manage to get one shot at it, then we might do it enough damage to slow it down enough to finish it off. So then, volunteers please?"

There was a pointed silence.

"It's like this," a skinny man with lank hair, the local banker, spoke up. "We're probably just going to stay here and wait for the army. I'm sure it's for the best."

"If the army are coming," said Leah. "That thing could

kill the lot of you before they get here. You need to defend yourselves."

"We'll wait for the army," said the banker, again. "They know what they're doing. No offence to you, mister," he said, to Shaule. "But we'll wait until your friends get here, I think."

There were murmurs of assent and nods of agreement from the villagers. "We need to defend the town. And we can't do it with just the two of us," said Leah.

"But it won't be the two of you once the army get here, will it?" said the Mayor.

"You're not going to help, are you?" said Leah, disdainfully. "You're going to let us sort it out for you, aren't you?"

"No," said the Mayor. "We're going to wait until professional help arrives. Load of us blundering around with hunting pieces, we're more likely to kill each other by mistake than kill this creature."

"How can you be so blind?" Leah shouted. "This thing is poisoning us even as we speak! My mother, my own mother is in the hospital. Most of you have friends, loved ones, even people you can't stand, all up there in the hospital. And this thing is to blame! Find it and the Sages can create an antidote. But whatever happens, we can't just stay here and pretend that there is nothing wrong!" Leah looked around the room, desperate for someone other than Shaule to side with her. "Oh, this is hopeless!"

"We're going nowhere," said the Mayor.

"A lock in!" said a gleeful voice from the bar "About time too! If the world's ending then I'm not facing it without a drink. Or several drinks, actually." It was Rendolph, a glass in each hand.

"Rendolph! I didn't see you. You've heard about Gim?" Leah rushed over to him.

"Oh yes. Good old Gim, stung by a worm and dying in hospital. Hate to say it, but you can see why some people might be a bit reluctant to go off monster hunting with you."

"What? No, you idiot, that's precisely why we have to go and find it!"

"So we can all get stung?"

"No! So we can stop it!"

"Stop it doing what?"

"Stop it killing the lot of us."

The Mayor coughed, meaningfully, and all eyes were on him again. "Yes, well, there we are then. All of us stay here until help arrives. The village has enough food and drink –"

"Hurray!" shouted Rendolph, raising his glass.

" – and we should all do the responsible thing and stay here until help arrives."

Shaule made for the door, shouldering his rifle. "The way I see it, there's one of me with a whole town to cover. Best thing to do is if I get to a high point and try and keep a look out for it. Don't know exactly what I'll do when I find it, mind."

"Perhaps you might try shooting it," said the banker.

"Thanks. I obviously hadn't thought of that," Shaule said and, with that comment, he was gone.

Leah watched the door close with a heavy heart. "Bollocks," she said. "Give me a drink."

"Castle Central to Patrol, come in please."

Krillan ran his fingers over his wrist-port. "Captain Krillan speaking. Receiving you Castle central." A picture swam into view. It was Rilston.

"Captain, we have a security breach on Castle Gate Four. We have reports from Sergeant Wallas that the post is deserted. You are required to head for Gate Nine at once and assess the situation."

"On my way." Krillan signalled to his patrol. As one, they made their way up the track towards the Castle walls.

Wallas was running. He had heard a sound from outside, and had carefully peeked around the doorway. To his horror, the worm had uncoiled itself from where it had been hiding in the undergrowth.

Not wasting a second, Wallas dropped to one knee and loosed a volley of shots at the creature's head. It snarled and spat a foul smelling green spray at him, but Wallas had already rolled to avoid it, cursing his creaking joints as he did so. He heard the sound of slithering behind him, but didn't stop until he reached the safety of a sentry box. Running into it, he turned and hurled a grenade. The creature arched its hideous body and the grenade exploded harmlessly yards away.

The worm rose to its full height, its tongue licking the air, smelling Wallas over the unfamiliar stench of the phosphor from the grenade.

Wallas only had one grenade left and only a small amount of ammunition. He reasoned, though, that he didn't have to kill the creature himself. He merely had to stay alive long enough for help to come.

He held the worm in his sites as it weaved from side to side. He saw its tongue flick back inside its mouth again and ducked back inside the sentry box as it projected another green mist at him.

As the creature lunged again, Wallas fired off three

rounds which smacked into the worm's scaly carapace. It made a hideous screeching noise, dropped and turned to face him, purple foam dripping from its teeth. It reared up over Wallas, who closed his eyes, expecting the end. But instead a loud booming explosion made him look up. The worm had been knocked sideways by a glancing shot from a small cannon. It was the smallest artillery piece currently in use by the Alleshi army, but the largest owned by the militia. Krillan had ordered the men drag it up the hill to the castle, and it was this that had wounded the creature.

"Fire at will!" shouted Krillan, and at once his men began to loose off rounds at the beast.

Wallas found a small depression in the ground and threw himself down into it, fearful of being accidentally hit by his comrades. Around him the ground erupted. Wallas held his breath, expecting at any moment to feel his flesh ripped apart.

"Cease firing!" It was Krillan's voice. "Cease firing."

Walls opened his eyes, rolled over and brought his weapon up to his shoulder.

There was no sign of the worm.

"Where is it?" he yelled to Krillan. "Where's it gone?"

"I don't know. It was here one moment and now it's gone. It just vanished."

"It can't have just vanished!"

"It's no use shouting at me Sergeant, I didn't make it disappear! I'd imagine we're looking at the possibility of a magic user being involved. Someone with the power to move things or people. Bloody wizards, you can't trust them an inch!" Krillan's men formed a loose circle, looking outward for any sign of the creature. "It was here one second and then it just wasn't," said Krillan, pulling a spike from his belt. "We need to track this thing, this spike will let us follow the trail of magical residue. The enchantment that made this thing disappear can be tracked."

Wallas rolled up his sleeve. "Give it here, Sir."

Krillan nodded and Wallas plunged the spike into his arm. His whole body stiffened as his eyes opened wide, suddenly seeing the world anew. He turned his back on the Castle. Looking at the residence of the Mage while full of this stuff could send a man mad. Instead he turned his gaze outward, to where they had fought the creature.

The air was full of magical particles. Tiny pinpricks of raw magic leading away from the Castle, and up towards the horizon. He could see the lines of energy in the sky left there by Holo Ships, the footprints on the ground left by one or two of the men, but of the creature there was no sign.

"Can't see anything. I'll have to turn round. It might be invisible. It could be hiding behind us."

Krillan clenched his jaw. "Alright, but be careful. Try not to look at the Castle directly if you can help it. The place is so overloaded with magic it could do you lasting harm while under the influence of this stuff."

Wallas turned. "I know the risks, sir." There in front of him, he saw the shadow of a worm, the afterimage picked out in bright red glitter, hanging in the air.

"I found it. It magicked out ten feet away. I should be able to get a trace."

Wallas walked towards the shimmering outline, that only he could see and cautiously prodding it with his bayonet. He was looking at the after-image of a magical transportation. The creature had transported itself. Turning slowly, he followed the magical path it had taken and saw the glittering trail that led towards the village.

"It's heading for the village."

Krillan put a hand on the Sergeant's shoulder.

"Thank you Sergeant, that'll do."

"But there's something else. I looked at the Castle. I looked at it full on. The home of the Mage. And I looked at it directly while pumped full of this stuff."

"We'll make sure you're looked after," said Krillan. "A couple of weeks rest and you'll be fine."

"No. You really don't understand. You see, I looked at the Castle and I felt nothing...." A tear trickled down Wallas' cheek. "I saw next to nothing. Captain, there's nothing there. There is hardly any magic left in the whole Castle!"

Krillan went pale, leaning closer to Wallas so as not to be overheard. "What? But how is that possible?"

"Either the magic has left the Mage, or else..." Wallas paused, trying to take it all in. "Or else the Mage is dead," he whispered.

"Sir! The village!" called one of the men.

The air was hazy, swimming. As Krillan looked, a bright line suddenly erupted along the ground in front of him. A thick bead of flame had ignited the grass, trees, everything that might be expected to burn, between him and the village.

"Heat barrier! He called back. "No one goes near it! Sergeant, contact the Castle, ask them what they're playing at."

"Whoever did this, it might not be the Castle. Maybe they hope to keep the creature separated from us?" said Wallas.

"Either way, we need to find out what's going on. Sergeant Wallas, I'll take half the squad and see if there's any way through that heat barrier. You take the rest and head on to the Castle, and see if we can't get some sensible answers to what's going on here."

The creature blinked into existence at the far end of the village, by the fishmonger's. It flinched, expecting attack. But when none came, it flicked its tongue out and, smelling life, roared in approval. Hearing the noise, the fishmonger's wife opened a window and leaned out. The worm shot forward and thrust its head in through the gap. The last thought the woman had before the darkness took her was that she was glad they had sent the children to the shelter.

The creature made its way along the street, sniffing its way from house to house, consuming life as it went.

The village blacksmith heard a noise and, running down the stairs, had the presence of mind to bring a hammer with him, in case it was an intruder. When the creature smashed its way in through the leadlight window in the parlour, he was prepared enough to strike the beast on the snout. He screamed out loud as he did so, repulsed by the hideous sight. The scream was enough for his wife to escape by climbing out onto the foundry roof that backed onto the rear of the house, clutching her two babies.

Private Shaule heard the scream and ran along the street, his weapon at the ready. He knew he should wait for support before tackling the creature alone, but then he heard the sound of crying children, which made up his mind for him. He kicked at the door of the blacksmith's house, which shrugged off his very best attempts at forced entry. The blacksmith, naturally enough, had the best bolts and locks in the whole village. Running round the back he saw the Blacksmith's wife, holding the babies on the roof of the forge. Through the open window he could see something thrashing about inside the house.

"Lower them to me. One at a time," said Shaule. "I won't drop them, I promise!"

"It's too far!" shrieked the woman.

Shaule looked round the yard, and felt a rush of adrenaline at the sight of the ladder lying near the shed. Picking it up he slammed it against the wall and climbed as fast as he could, his heart racing.

He emptied his backpack of everything. Medi-kit, rations, every single item he had been drilled into keeping good care of.

"Here, quick," Shaule said. "They'll be safe." Gently, but with haste, the placed the two screaming children in his backpack, swung it round over his front, and slid down the ladder, burning his hands as he did so.

"Now!" he called to the blacksmith's wife, "Quickly, come down."

She hoisted her skirt, and started to climb down the ladder just as the creature loomed over her. Shaule loosed off three shots straight at its face. The babies screamed at the noise, but thankfully the thing ducked away, out of sight. Grabbing the woman's hand, Shaule ran towards the Inn. "My husband's in there!" wailed the woman.

"I'm sorry," said Shaule. "There's nothing I can do. You need to take care of the children. They need you to be brave. As brave as your husband was."

Reaching the Inn, Shaule banged on the door with his rifle butt. "Open up!" he yelled. "Open up now!" The door swung open and Shaule pushed the woman with the babies inside before following them in.

"It's outside," said Shaule, out of breath. "What are we going to do?"

"Well," said the Mayor, "I think we should –"
"I wasn't talking to you!" Shaule snapped. "Leah! What do we do?"

Everyone looked at Leah. Suddenly aware of the weight of so many pairs of eyes, Leah did the only sane thing left to her. She knocked back her drink in one. "Right," she said. "Here's the plan."

Grefno was back in the Castle library, pouring over his books of spells. He had commandeered every sprite and Pixie he could find to help him. The air was full of tiny creatures as they carried books and scrolls from one level of the bookshelves to the next. The air hung thick with dust from disturbed volumes.

He had tried to get Niaal to help him, but his friend could not be found.

His eyes closed, he was viewing pages through the eyes of five separate Pixies as they flicked through five different volumes.

Worms. Everything about worms he could get his hands on. Their strengths, weaknesses, likes, habits, everything he could find.

"Grefno! Honoured Sage!" It was his guards, the Chemical Warriors, standing on the floor of the library, far below him. "Honoured Sage, we have an urgent message for you, Sir."

"I'm busy!" shouted Grefno, his eyes still clenched shut in concentration.

"Sir! The message is most urgent. It comes from Captain Krillan, of the militia. He insists you respond to it."

Grefno leaped up from the leather armchair he had been working from, and hurled himself over the balcony into the air. The sprites caught him at once, snagging his robes in their tiny fingers, as they gently lowered him to the ground where the soldiers were. They looked at him, stunned.

"Come on then!" shouted Grefno, running towards the

door. "We haven't got all day!"

With worried glances to each other, his guards ran after him.

Grefno came into the central courtyard at a gallop, nearly knocking over the blue armoured Castle guards that tried to open the door for him. "Where's Krillan?" he shouted.

A junior officer in immaculate blue uniform pointed to a mirror, hanging in the air. "Managed to get the comms working again, sir. The captain is on this line, and insists he speaks to you and no one else."

"Right. Everyone out of my way." He brushed the mirror with his finger. "Go ahead, captain." Krillan's face swum into view. His hair was in disarray and there were beads of sweat running down his cheeks.

"Sage! The worm, it's here! It somehow managed to kill the perimeter guards. Sergeant Wallas followed it here and we managed to scare it off. We're fairly sure it's gone to the village."

"Is Wallas still with you?" said Grefno, pulling phials and potions from his belt, hidden beneath his robes.

"He's heading back to the Castle. He took a Reveal Spike and looked at the Castle. Grefno, Wallas said he couldn't see anything."

Grefno's face went white. "I see..."

"Is there anyone else you can send to help us?"

"Yes. Yes, of course. I'll have the another Sage come at once, as soon as I find him. Everyone else is off on bloody stupid expeditions along our borders, gearing up for the war."

"Fine. Sooner rather than later would be good. Krillan out." With that the screen went blank.

Grefno turned to face his guards. "Please inform the esteemed Sage Niaal that he is needed as a matter of urgency. The rest of you follow me. We need an audience with the Mage."

The Chemical Warriors looked at each other, daring the other to speak.

"With respect, honoured Sage," said one. "But protocol insists that you may only address the Mage when directly summoned."

"By the Mage," piped up the other.

"Thank you, gentlemen," Grefno said, still striding onwards. "I am quite aware of Castle protocol and I thank you for your concern. I think you will find that I am right in saying that a Sage can address the Mage directly, without council permission in matters of extreme urgency. Now then, I'd love to debate the issue of what constitutes 'extreme' urgency with you, but I'd say that half the village dead or dying, and a giant magical creature attacking the Castle walls is probably a fair example of what might be classed as an extreme measure."

CHAPTER NINE

The Castle rippled.

Grefno was knocked from his feet, falling in an ungainly heap, twisted in his robes. His retinue of Chemical Warriors drew their weapons in alarm, unsure whether the phenomenon was real or imagined. Rising to his feet, Grefno leaned against a wall for support, and as he did so he felt his hand sink into the stonework. Quickly he pulled his hand out, startled.

What was this?

Either he had taken on the strength of a hundred men, which was unlikely, or else... he pressed his hand against the wall again, but it held firm. He banged it with his fist but, again, nothing. The wall was solid. Closing his eyes, Grefno allowed his mind to run over the wall, searching for any signs of magical weakness. There was nothing.

"What is it, Sir?" said the warrior whose job it was to never take his eyes from him. "What just happened?"

"I don't know," said Grefno. "Nothing good, that much we can gather. Come on, let's keep moving."

In the Garden, the corporal in charge of the work detail left his men on guard, watching the village for signs of movement, but nothing stirred. The gunfire they had heard earlier was not repeated and all was now quiet and still.

"Anything from the Castle yet?" The Corporal asked the comms operator.

He shook his head, gloomily. "Nothing. They came up briefly, but they've gone again. They say they're looking into it, but you know what they're like up there."

The corporal, rubbed his wrist, wondering why the stream of updates had ground to a halt, why could they no longer access any of the standard comms channels from the Castle? What was going on up there?

"Right lads, we're getting nowhere standing round like this. How much can you see up there?" he yelled to the men high up in the fungi.

"Nothing, Corp. No movement at all in the village."

"What about the Castle?"

"Doesn't look like there's anything wrong to me."

"Right. I don't know what's going on in the village, but we need to find out. I want two of you to make a break for that ditch over there." He pointed to a deep furrow about a hundred yards off. "We'll cover you the whole way, just in case. As soon as you get there and signal all safe we'll send two more to go past you to the road down to the village, and from there up to the Castle. The lads in the ditch will watch out for you until you're out of sight. And don't forget the assault rifle upstairs." He pointed to the platform high on the side of the mushroom. "They'll be able to see you the whole time, so you'll be alright. Any trouble, anything at all, you run back here at the double. Alright?"

Cautiously, the two troopers made their way towards the ditch, each covering the other as they had been taught. Their weapons primed, and with full sensor sweeps of the area, they moved at a steady pace. Reaching cover, one of them signalled back to the Garden wall, and two more troopers came out, at a faster pace, now that they knew the ground between them and the ditch had been made safe. Moving beyond the two in the ditch, they made their way down the track that connected the Gardens to the village.

Nothing stirred. The two soldiers looked at each other. What were they supposed to be looking for? With a glance back towards the men in the ditch, they set off towards the village.

The corporal watched them make their way around the corner, and then out of sight. He shouted up to the couple with the assault rile. "Can you still see them?"

"Yes, Corp. Road looks clear. Don't worry, anything funny starts moving, anything at all, then we'll shovel high-ex at it until it stops."

"Alright. But make sure you get a look at it first. Don't want you shooting civilians, do we?"

The corporal waved to the two men in the ditch to move on and take up new positions. Hoping he hadn't just sent two men to their deaths, he ran back to check the comms links again.

One of the soldiers fired his weapon twice and then twice again, the prearranged signal to his comrades in the Garden that they had reached their destination. Nervous, the two men headed off down the cobbled road for the Castle. They were about half a mile from the first perimeter wall when they ran into the heat barrier. A line of scorched grass ran either side of the road, which was now blurring in the haze of an intense heat. One of the soldiers picked up a clump of dry grass and threw it towards the haze. It flared briefly in the heat. They looked at each other, startled. The Castle was cut off. Whatever help was to be had, it would not be coming from there.

That is, unless it was the Castle itself who needed helping? As they watched, they saw movement on the far side of the heat barrier. Men coming towards them. They saw that it was a mixed group of Castle guards, together with one or two in the brown armour of the militia. They saluted Captain Krillan as soon as he swam into sight thorough the haze.

The Captain was obviously saying something, but the heat barrier seemed to absorb sound as well. In fact, the closer they got to it, they noticed it made a deep rumbling sound.

They held their hands to their ears, letting the men on the other side know that they could not hear them.

"What are they doing?" snapped one of the Castle guards, irritably.

"They're saying they can't hear us," said Krillan. "That right, men?" Nothing came back. "Must be a by-product of the heat barrier." He turned to the guard, who had first spoken, "Do you have your flashlight with you, soldier?"

The guard pulled his torch from his belt. "Yes, Sir."

"Good. Transcribe for me." The operator began flicking the light on and off at the two men, turning Krillan's words into the coded alphabet used by all soldiers in the field as a last resort. Pulling a pen and paper from his pocket, one of the two militia men began writing down the code, letter by letter, his comrade peering over his shoulder as the words took form.

Back in the Inn, Leah heard the gunshots from the soldiers outside, and ran to the window. "What was that?" she said.

"Signal," said Shaule. "It's a militia sign."

The small woman clapped her hands together in delight. "Then we are saved!"

"Not necessarily," said Leah. "You don't think it could be them shooting at the worm, or something?"

"It could, but it's unlikely. The timed shots like that, we're trained to do that. If it was the creature then we'd have heard more, I'd say."

"Unless it has killed them too," said the Mayor.

Leah glared at him. "Yes. Well, thank you for that cheerful thought. Either way, it means that there are people moving around outside, and we should probably go and find them. If they're in trouble then they'll be safer here with us. If there's a lot of them, or if they're very well armed, then we'd be safer off out there with them."

Rendolph went over to the window, peering out cautiously.

"How about if we stay safe in here, and they stay heavily armoured out there, guarding us with their lives?"

Shaule sniffed, contemptuously. "Is your friend a coward?"

Leah and Rendolph looked at each other. "Yes," they chorused, together.

"Come on, whatever's going on, we're better off out there knowing what it is. Rendolph, you come with us."

"Do I have to?"

"No."

"Thank you."

Leah smiled. "No, just kidding. Rendolph you're coming with us. The rest of you carry on as you were."

Leah opened the door of the Inn and screamed.

The worm was outside. Rearing up to its full height, ready to strike, it hissed a foul cloud of vapour towards

Leah, who froze to the spot, terrified at what might come next. Rendolph grabbed her by her collar and pulled her back into the Inn. "Close the door!" shouted Shaule, raising his rifle to the firing position. Rendolph threw himself at the door, slamming it shut as Leah threw the bolt across.

"It was outside!" whispered Rendolph in terror.

"Apparently so," said Leah.

"No, but it was outside. Waiting for us!" said Rendolph, backing away from the door.

"Yes. We've agreed on that," said Leah. "Worm. Door. Us." She turned to Shaule. "You said you could communicate by bursts of gunfire. Can't you do that now and have a chat with your pals out there?"

Shaule checked the weapon, grimacing. "I could, but I'm a bit low on ammo. I think we're better off conserving it. Besides, they'll have heard the commotion and will come running to have a look, I wouldn't wonder. We're better off where we are, I'd say."

There was a crash as the large saloon window burst inwards, sending shards of glass flying across the room. The townsfolk recoiled in panic.

"On the other hand, maybe there's something to be said for being outside," said Shaule.

A tall, long haired man suddenly screamed, his chest fountaining blood, as the creature thrust its viciously barbed tail in through the window, spearing him and lifting him off his feet. In the midst of the panic, Leah found herself calmly noticing just how lucky Gim had been with his injury. The beast flicked its tail, and the impaled man was sent flying across the room, slamming into the bar. The tail darted sideways again, looping another man around the waist. The creature jerked the man upwards, snapping his head on the ceiling, before dropping him like a heavy sack. Again the tail flashed across the room and Shaule slashed at it with his bayonet. A deep gash appeared in its greasy skin, accompanied by a hissing, roaring sound. The tail disappeared through the window.

"You hurt it!" shouted Leah, approvingly, her eyes full of admiration. The heavy door buckled and splintered as the creature slammed against it in anger, trying to bash its way in from the street.

"Everyone in the cellar!" yelled the barman.

"No!" shouted Shaule. "We'll be trapped in there"

"We're already trapped in here!" shouted Rendolph.

With a boom like a cannon going off, the door was wrenched from its hinges. Quick as a cat, the worm poured itself into the room and wrapped itself around Leah, pinning her arms to her side. She screamed, staring at Rendolph in stark terror.

Shaule whipped something from his equipment belt and slapped it directly into the open bayonet wound on the beast's flesh. At once the room filled with bright red smoke and the worm withdrew, twisting Leah like a spinning top, and sending her flying into Rendolph's arms.

"What was that?" Rendolph said.

"Distress flare. Best thing I could think of," said Shaule. "I imagine it's quite painful, burning away like that in an already open wound. Hopefully we've driven it off for now. Trouble is, the street is so full of smoke that I can hardly see a thing. I think it best if we find somewhere else to hide. It knows this place, and knows it can get in again any time it feels like it. We need somewhere stronger." He threw a half smile at Rendolph. "It's alright, we'll bring some carry-outs with us."

Krillan read the translation on the paper in front of him one more time and then turned to face the soldier who had transcribed it for him.

"This is magic we're up against," he said. "This is magic, and we're out of our depth." He rubbed his eyes, suddenly tired.

Another soldier ran up, a bulky wooden frame on his back, from which hung a silk screen.

"Sir! Found this in the guardroom. It's an old model and looks like it's still working!" The soldier placed the wooden frame in front of Krillan and began to make signs with his hands in the air. As he did so an image took shape on the screen. It was one of the comms officers in the Castle. The image was blurry and kept fading in and out but would be good enough for now.

"Castle, this is Captain Krillan! Can you hear me?"

"Go ahead Captain."

"Castle, please put me through to the Sage Grefno as a matter of urgency."

"Putting you through, Captain." The screen flickered as the image swam in front of them. "Better keep it brief, sir. Don't know how long this thing will hold."

"What's wrong with it?" snapped Krillan. "Can it be fixed?"

"Hard to say sir. It's an antique." The man smiled. "That's the army for you. Never throw anything away without an order in writing."

The screen swirled once more and the unmistakable figure of Grefno appeared, his yellow robes glowing like sunflowers.

"Yes Captain? What's the situation out there?"

"We can't get through to the village. There's some kind of heat barrier stopping us. We've been contacted by two members of the militia who've made their way up from the Garden. They say the village appears empty, so we're guessing the villagers are in hiding."

"Or else they're already dead. And what of the worm?"

"According to Wallas, it seems to be able to blink in and out of existence. That means that even though the barrier might keep us out, there's no guarantee that it will work on the creature. Any news from the Mage?"

"I'm trying to get word to the Mage, but it's not as easy as you'd think."

Krillan smiled. "I'm sure no one thinks it's easy."

"I'll find a way to raise the heat barrier from here, Captain. As soon as it lifts, you move your men and try and get the people from village evacuated and bring them all back to the Castle."

"And the men in the Garden, sir?"

"If there are any left alive when you get there, get them to help with the evacuation. Good luck."

The picture flared briefly like the mantle on a gas lamp, and then was gone.

In the Castle, Grefno closed his eyes and collected his thoughts once again. The Castle was now effectively cut off from the outside world. Walking along the corridor, Grefno felt a sudden pain in his wrist, as if the arteries in his arm had suddenly hardened, spasming with a sharp burning sensation.

Reaching out with his mind, Grefno realised that he was now cut off from the within-body link that so many of his people shared. He was truly alone. Turning a corner he saw a group of blue uniformed Castle guards, similarly rubbing their wrists with alarm. "Sir," called one. "We've lost links to the network. We can't open them up again."

"Me too," said Grefno. "Something's brought the whole thing crashing down. Please consider yourselves on high alert. Inform the highest ranking officer you can find, and then tell him to alert the highest ranking officer he can find."

Things were getting worse. The war seemed to have started a day early, though it was not them who had made the first strike.

It was time to see the Mage.

CHAPTER TEN

There were no guards in the ante-chamber. There should have been a phalanx of Castle guards on constant watch on the approaches to the Mage's quarters, but instead the room was deserted. Grefno stood there, suddenly unsure of what to do next. He had approached the Mage countless times, and on each occasion the guards had challenged him. Their non-appearance was greatly disturbing. Edging forward, he felt outwards with the invisible arts of the magician. He stretched his consciousness, feeling his way around the room as he looked for traps and snares, devices that would be hidden to the uninitiated mind of anyone below the rank of Sage. There was nothing. The place was clean.

Opening the doors to the anteroom he entered the outer chamber. This again was deserted. He was within metres of the holiest place in the Castle, no, the entire state, and was deeply disturbed to find that he had not been challenged or questioned. He crossed the ornamental bridge that traversed the plasma flowing out from the Mages' chamber. Normally it would have been alive with energy, sparkling with beauty as it carried out the by-products of magic.

Looking down, he could that see it was brown.

Grefno braced himself before entering the Mage's chamber. So intense, so wonderful was the power of the Mage, that it could do strange things to the mind. Grefno, like everyone else who had to enter the chamber regularly, had undergone extensive training to prevent himself being swamped by the sheer wonder of it all.

He pushed his hand into the mouth of the brass face that was mounted on the door, feeling the sterile dart slide into his wrist-port, recognising him and interrogating him, before decided whether to open the portal or to inject him with a lethal dose of poison.

The face winked and the door opened with a deep, woody creak, like a mighty oak swaying in a strong breeze. Taking a deep breath, Grefno strode into the room.

The Mage's chamber should have been full of light. The room itself should have radiated the creativity, the sheer joyous magical will of the Mage.

Instead, it was dark. Dark and cold. He could hear his footsteps echoing in the gloomy chamber.

On his last visit, he had been held in his tracks by the sound of the thought chimes that tinkled and stroked his consciousness. There had been wonderful music that you heard with you soul and your heart as much as with your ears, that played harmonics on your nerve endings and pitched it's rhythm to that of your own heartbeat.

The Mage was everything to Grefno. The life of the Mage, the very idea of the Mage was so deeply ingrained within him that to suddenly find himself standing in this echoing and empty darkness was an appalling shock.

"Mage?" he whispered. "It is Grefno. The Sage." Nothing came back. Nothing but the echo of his own voice.

Stroking the air in front of him with the barest suggestion of a hand movement, he dared to create a small magical ball of light. It flickered briefly and then went out. Again he tried. This time the ball burned brighter, flaring brightly before it too again withered to nothing. His hands shaking Grefno tore of a strip from his cloak, and tied it around one of the pendants he wore under his robes, holding it aloft, he tapped the pendant with his forefinger. As he did so, the material burst into flames, but this time it did not go out. He could now see the marble floor in front of him, but little else. The darkness seemed to grow, to become all the more solid around him.

He closed his eyes, trying to picture himself in the room he had visited so many time before, but it was hard when so many of his memories were of the lights, the beautiful scents and sounds that filled the Mage's chamber. He realised that he couldn't picture himself in the room in his mind, because he could not actually picture it ever being dark.

Looking down he noticed the pattern on the floor, and suddenly gained his bearings once again. He was standing on a mosaic, an intricately patterned image of the sea. Like all who entered the Mage's chamber and wished to keep their sanity, he had learned to avert his gaze from the Mage himself. In doing so he now knew every inch of the floor pattern by heart.

Working from right to left, his tracked the path of the dolphins on the floor until they met the sea monsters. This was his clue to turn to his right and follow the shoals of tiled fish until he came to the image of the giant crab in the centre of the room. The Mage's throne should now be twenty feet straight in front of him.

Walking slowly across the floor, using the pattern of the fish as a guide, he advanced to where the Mage should be seated.

The light should have been pouring out of the Mage by this point. To his disquiet, the closer he approached the throne, the more intense the dark became.

The thin light from his pendant caught something up ahead. At first he grasped at hope, assuming it to be some faint magical trace, some glimmer from the Mage. But it was not.

He was looking at a reflection of the light. He was

standing looking at a shiny, curved surface. Raising the light he saw that the entire throne was surround by what looked for all the world like a bubble. A film of some constant moving liquid, like a dirty soap bubble, only twenty feet high.

He felt ill. The throne was completely surrounded by the disgusting membrane like a huge balloon, like an egg sack.

Egg sack.

"Oh no." He stepped closer, horrified. "Oh no." He came closer to the viscous film, breathing through his mouth against the vile smell.

The sacred space of the Mage was alive.

It moved, it bulged and squirmed. The entire egg was in motion, a brown, hideous mass of movement.

The egg was alive. With worms. Dropping the torch, Grefno jumped backwards in disgust. "Mage..." He said, his voice a whisper. "Mage, what has happened to you?"

He watched, repulsed as the egg sac bulged. The hideous creatures within slithered and slid though the vile liquid.

Grefno backed towards the door, never once taking his eyes from the abomination. "Guards!" He shouted. "Guards, inside now!" But no footsteps came. There was nothing except the sound of his own beating heart and the tap of his shoes on the marble floor.

Still facing the abomination, he cast a quick glance past the entrance. The guards were nowhere to be seen. He was alone.

It was insane. This was the most magically powerful place in all of Allesh. There should be guards everywhere, Sages and palace staff attending to the Mage's every need.

Approaching the door, he placed his hand into a communications port, allowing him access to the Castle internal combinations systems. Normally the Castle bureaucracy was humming with civil servants and officials, carrying out the will of the Mage, administering the state in his name.

Changing frequencies he tried the Castle guard themselves, but again received nothing but white noise. It was as if something had eaten the communication network within the Castle.

There was no response from Castle transportation, nor from the hangers that maintained and ordered the Thought Ships and aircraft. Nothing from the stables, nothing from any of the security stations.

He finally accessed the security web, showing him the movements of everyone in the Castle.

He felt sweat run cold on his brow as he saw the results. According to the report, he was the only human in this entire wing of the castle. Sages, Warriors, servants, all were missing.

Grefno leaned against the wall, never once letting his eyes slip from the hideous egg shape before him. As he stood there, his mind racing with possibilities, he was startled by a sudden blip of contact from the screen.

It was the hospital. Someone from the hospital was picking up his signal.

"This is Grefno." He spoke the words, in a careful measured tone that belied his fear.

"Grefno? This is Doctor Barrot. What in the nine hells is going on? We're losing power in the hospital."

"Doctor Barrot! A pleasure to hear a familiar voice." Grefno took a breath. "The situation is in the Castle is... complicated. I'm afraid that we need your help."

"You need our help? Grefno, have you any idea how many patients we're dealing with here? There are dying people on stretchers lined up in every corridor on both floors. Every store room larger than a cupboard is now classified as a ward. And you need our help?" Kadia Barrot paused, watching her husband on the far side of the ward as he closed the lifeless eyes of a middle-aged man. It was Felson, the owner of the shoe shop. She had kissed him once when they were teenagers.

"The Castle seems to have suffered some attacked from within." Grefno said. "I am not sure what has happened to the Mage."

"What do you mean you're not sure? Have you been to see him?"

"I think I have seen him. It's hard to tell. As I said, things here are... complicated."

"Grefno, you've either seen the Mage or you haven't. Surely it's s straightforward as that." Kadia's voice tailed off. "Isn't it?"

"I don't know. I've been into the chamber and I've stood in front of the throne, but I don't know if I've seen the Mage or not."

"Then what did you see?"

"Worms."

"Worms? In the Mage's chamber?"

Grefno pulled himself together, concentrating on what to say next. "Leah Carleaf, one of the Gardeners thought she saw a creature in the well. We have identified the creature as a Gentle Worm, a species native to the Hirvan wastes. They secrete a toxic slime. If this beast has been living in the well, then it's more than likely that it's been poisoning us."

"So why do some have the sickness and not others?" said Kadia.

"Some people drink more water than others. Possibly the poison is concentrated the nearer you get to the source. That's my guess at least. The toxin is almost

certainly magically aggravated, so it probably follows
its own rules to a certain extent. It is fair to say that
the illness won't be behaving in a normal, conventional
sense. There is a possibility that those affected could even
be linked to the creature in some way."

"What do you mean?"

"Hirvan worms can influence and control some other
life forms. Plants, in the main. But if it has the ability
to reach out and control other organisms, then there is
a chance that it could have linked in some way to the
victims of the poisoning."

Doctor Barot paused, trying to take it all in. "Can you
catch it, Grefno? Can you get a sample of the creature so
that an antidote can be created?"

"I hope so. In the meanwhile, do your best. The hospital
has its own water supply, doesn't it, doctor?"

"It does. It's fed from the stream that flows along from
the woods. Just as well, by the sound of it, Grefno."

"Indeed. I will call you as soon as I have further news,
doctor. Grefno out."

Leaving the Mage's chamber and the abomination that
pulsated and bulged at its centre, Grefno made his way
towards the library. He felt naked without his guards, and
was becomingly increasingly worried.

The Inn was quiet. The door and window which had
previously been subjected to a constant battering by the
worm, had now been reinforced by piling chairs and
furniture against them. Since Shaule had attacked it with
the burning flare, the worm had not been seen or heard.

"Perhaps it's given up?" said the innkeeper, a broken
bottle in each shaking hand, his eyes never leaving the

broken window.

"It's always possible," said Leah. "Or else it's doing something else."

"Like what?" said Rendoplh.

"Well I don't know! Something nasty, probably. Some nasty, wormy things."

Shaule stood up, addressing the occupants of the room. "We need to find somewhere else to hide, and which can be better defended. Any ideas?"

"How about the barracks?" said the innkeeper. "I would have thought that would be the safest place, no?"

"We've already been there once today, " said Leah. "We're not going back again."

"Leah's right," said Shaule. "We need to find somewhere else before the worm comes back."

Rendolph stood up, placing his ear to the wall at the back of the room. "Hey! Can everyone keep quiet for a bit?" The people in the room turned to look at him as he stood side on to the wall, straining to hear something on the other side. "Come and listen to this."

"What is it?" said the innkeeper, joining him.

"Don't know. Some kind of scratching sound."

"Stand back," said Shaule. "Really, get away from the wall now!" Rendolph did as he was told at once, joining Shaule and Leah in the middle of the room, but the innkeeper stayed with his ear pressed to the wall.

"It could be rescuers!" said the innkeeper. "Perhaps they've come to get us at last." He turned to smile at them. "Honestly, you people. Have you no faith at all?"

The smile was still on his face when, with a deafening roar, the wall bulged, collapsing inwards. The falling wooden beams and plaster caught the innkeeper, knocking him to the ground. Above him, triumphant in rage, towered the worm. It opened its slime-crusted jaws and bit the innkeeper clean in half.

Backing away with the rest of the villagers, Leah grabbed Rendolph by his collar and ran towards the door. "Help me!" she shouted, throwing chairs across the room as she pulled the barricade apart.

Shaule knew he had to buy them time to get the barricade down. While the creature was busy with the innkeeper, then the others were at least safe for the moment, and so he held his fire. There was, he reasoned, no point in antagonising the beast in an enclosed space, not when there were so many people in the room. He waited until the beast had finished with the innkeeper before he raised his rifle and fired.

With a hiss, the creature turned about and flicked its tail across the room.

"This way!" shouted Leah, pulling the last chair away from in front of the door. "Run!"

The villagers needed no further encouragement and were soon outrunning her down the high street. Glancing over her shoulder Leah saw to her horror that the creature, having finally been forced away from the rear of the building by Shaule's gunfire, was now coming around the side towards them. "This way!" she shouted to Rendolph. "Inside the bakery, quick!"

The two friends ran into the bakery, slamming the door after them. They stood there panting, their backs to the door.

"You think it's noticed us?" Rendolph asked. "It might have been scared off by the shooting."

He was answered by a crash of glass as the creature thrust its head in to the tiny shop. Up close, Leah could see bits of the innkeeper's clothes stuck to its glistening teeth.

"Yes, I think it noticed us!" Leah shouted, running.

As they reached the rear of the shop, the worm lunged towards them, its mouth open in a savage snarl. As it did so, Leah flung open the doors to the oven, pushing Rendolph to one side as she went to the other. The heat was intense, as the ovens had been burning dangerously out of control for some hours now, whilst the baker sheltered in the inn. With a squeal of pain, the creature recoiled away from the heat, hissing and spitting as it retreated from the shop in search of easier game.

"Ouch!" said Leah, kicking the doors shut with her boots. She turned to her friend. "You all right?"

He smiled weakly. "Not really. There's this buggering great wormy dragon thing trying to eat us. It's kind of upset me." He sat down heavily. "I'd quite like to be sick now."

Leah picked up a sweet bun from one of the shelves and took a bite. "Come on," she said. "Got to keep your strength up, you know."

At the castle, Wallas checked the safety catch on his weapon, slid a performance enhancing ampoule into his wrist-port to make him sharp, and then went on through the main gate. The two militiamen with him looked from side to side, still unsure that they should even be here, yet alone looking for trouble.

Rounding a corner they saw the first bodies. Blue uniformed Castle guards, slumped to the floor. They had large wounds on their chests where the worm had lashed out with its tail. One or two had bite marks on their faces.

"Is this what the worm does to you?" said one of the soldiers.

"Looks like it," said Wallas. "But just because these were regulars, doesn't mean that we're any easier to kill. They weren't expecting trouble; we are. You got that, boys?"

"Yes, Sarge."

"Good. Now down the corridor, one door at a time and keep alert. Anything moves, try and shout out first before shooting. We don't want to do our own boys, do we?"

Moving further in to the Castle they found technicians, administrators, cleaning staff, all of them with the same wounds. In one wing they found yellow clad Chemical Warriors lying next to Sages. All dead.

Wallas checked the readouts on his armour. There was no sign of radiation or chemical and biological attack. His amulet that warned of magical weaponry was going berserk, however. Although they had some defences against magical attack, it wasn't their area of expertise by a long margin.

He bent down to retrieve two more magical amulets from two dead Chemical Warriors. He handed them to his companions. "Here. Better than nothing."

The men climbed the immense marble staircase that flowed upwards from the entrance hall, passing more dead bodies as they did so. Wallas came to a halt, checking his sensor readings. "We've got life signs up ahead."

"Survivors?"

"Could be. Either that or we've found the target."

Cautiously, the three men rounded the corner at the top of the staircase. They passed more bodies, this time in the yellow of Chemical Warriors. The life signs led them towards a panelled door.

"It's locked, sir," said one of the soldiers. "Looks like it's jammed. Mechanism has been interfered with."

"Right. Let's open it then," said Wallas. Carefully, one of the soldiers placed an explosive charge against the door mechanism. They took cover, their hands over their ears as the device was detonated.

Rushing around the corner, weapons at the ready, they burst into the dark room. The flashlights on their impulse projector barrels searched for a target in the smoke filled room. A sudden movement caused them all to raise their weapons and shout out a challenge.

"Stay where you are!" Wallas shouted.

A Sage stood in front of them, his hands in the air, a look of terror on his face. It looked as if he had been crying.

"Please don't shoot! I'm a Sage! My name is Niaal."

Grefno had also found bodies as he made his way towards the library. He was passing by the armoury when a noise from within made him stop and turn. Cautiously he entered the high vaulted stone annex.

Following the noise of movement he saw an officer, dragging himself across the floor. It was Rilston, the Captain of the guard. "Rilston! Stay there, I'm coming over," Grefno called out.

"Keep back! I think I'm infected!"

"It's not an infection, Rilston. It's a poison. You can't catch it from other people," said Grefno. "It's a worm poison, semi-magical in nature. It's been poisoning people for weeks through the water supply."

"It stung me, Grefno. The worm has this spike on the end of its tail and it stung me," Rilston coughed. "We were trying to fight it off, but it was hopeless. I managed to put my armour on, hoping it would give enough protection against a direct strike from the tail. Seemed a good idea as any."

"Good thinking." Grefno said, checking Rilston's injuries

whilst trying not to let on quite how badly wounded the officer was. "It's probably what kept you alive." Grefno eyed the suits of armour lined up on the wall, following them along until he spotted a Chemical Warrior's yellow suit. It had been a long while since he'd had to wear one, but it was easy enough to recall how it was done.

"How long have you been lying here?" he asked, trying to make Rilston as comfortable as possible. "When did the beast strike?"

"I don't know. I think I must have passed out when I was hit. It might be an idea to armour yourself up by the way."

Grefno slid into the armour. As he felt the inner body suit cling to him, the sensors reached into his limbs, augmenting them and making him feel twenty years younger. "You're lucky to be alive, Captain. Forgive me for asking, but is it anything more than luck that has protected you?"

"I'm working for the Mage. Directly reporting to him alone. He has been concerned for some time that there was a plot against him, although he had no real evidence to go on, beyond his own magical predictions." Rilston coughed again. "I was seconded from the navy by the Mage himself, brought in to specifically investigate goings on in the castle. The illness caused the Mage to be greatly alarmed."

"I see. Well, it appears the Mage's fears were well founded, Rilston. Tell me, have you seen the Mage recently?"

"No. As security was tightened I found that I had been denied access to him along with everyone else. He will now only talk to the Sage Niaal."

"And he left you no way of communicating with him? No secret transmitter or anything like that?"

"The Mage furnished me with many tools to help. They all stopped working two weeks ago. I have been out of contact with the Mage since then. I do not know what has happened to him. I naturally fear the worst,"whispered Rilston. Grefno knelt by the man, adjusting the settings on his armour to try and take the pain away. "I was concerned that he might have caught the illness. The thought occurred to me that he might be ill, and the Sages were keeping it quiet."

"I think the Mage is dead, Rilston."

"What do you mean, you 'think' he's dead? Have you seen a body?"

"I... I don't know. I have seen something, but whether or not it is still the Mage I cannot say with certainty. Tell me, did the Mage have any views on the illness that he might have shared with you? Anything at all?"

"Listen, the illness is somehow magical in nature and has unexpected side effects. If the Mage is infected, then the illness will almost certainly mutate into a new strain, transmitted magically. It could infect those with whom the Mage is in constant communion."

"You mean the other Mages? But that would mean..." Grefno's voice tailed off, horrified at his own thoughts.

"It would mean the end of peace. It would mean that there would no longer be the comfort of mutually assured magical destruction holding Inan together." Rilston held Grefno's appalled gaze. "It would mean the start of a new war." Rilston coughed, his face pale as snow. "Find him, Grefno. Find him and stop him." Then he was gone.

Another sound from outside made Grefno turn. If Rilston was to be believed, then whoever was responsible for this madness may still be at large in the Castle. Closing Rilston's eyes, Grefno turned and ran down the corridor in front of him. Passing a control panel, he activated the emergency seal, bring a shield down in the corridor behind him. He came to a halt outside his personal office, a defensive spell readied at his fingertips. Cautiously entering, he was relieved to find the room empty.

He ran to his chair and opened a concealed compartment. He dragged a case from the bottom, tools he'd had hidden for such a day as this. Slinging the case over his shoulders, he gave one last look around the room and headed out into the corridor.

Whatever had attacked the people of Allesh, the Castle had fallen to it. For Grefno to stand any chance of defeating the threat he would have to gather what troops he could find, and regroup. The longer he was in the Castle, the more likely it was that he would succumb to the horror that roamed its corridors.

Feeling his heart about to burst, Grefno ran to an ornate stained glass window and, without a second's thought, hurled himself though it. Instantly his armour shielded him from the shattering glass. With a jolt, a silk parachute unfurled from his back. The ground rushed up to meet him – not the best landing ever. But then, he had just survived a fall from one hundred and thirty feet straight up.

Pulling the harness from him as fast as he could, Grefno set off towards the group of soldiers who had ran towards him as soon as they had seen him crash out of the Castle. Captain Krillan was watching in disbelief, mouth open. "We need to get away, Captain. The Castle's done for," said Grefno.

"That was amazing!" said Krillan.

"Airborne assault troops," said Grefno. "I served with them as a Chemical Warrior for five years, during the war. Thankfully none of my former colleagues are here to laugh at my undignified landing today."

Leah looked out of the window of the bakery. Across the street, by the well, was a transport, a small utility vehicle used to deliver milk and groceries.

"How fast do you think that thing is, Rendolph?" said Leah. "Do you think it could outrun the worm?"

"Why? You thinking of making a run for it?"

"No. I was wondering if we could lure it away from the village. Use ourselves as bait."

"Well, we're only trapped with no weapons and a monstrous slavering beast outside trying to eat us! But let's see if we can put ourselves in even more danger!"

"I only asked," said Leah, sniffily. She looked up and down the street again. "I wonder if any of the horses survived."

"Leah, will you stop it!"

"Well we can't just stay here for the rest of our lives."

"I know that. It's just if we go outside, then 'The rest of our lives' as you put it will be measured in minutes, not years!"

"I suppose you're right."

"I am right. Now come away from the window, before it sees you again."

Grefno and Krillan were leading the men down the hill towards the heat barrier and the village. After a brief discussion they had decided that the only course of action was to try and find the worm. They left a detail of men at the Castle gate, to wait for Sergeant Wallas, whilst the rest followed the Captain and the Sage down towards the village.

"What do we do about the heat barrier?" asked

Krillan.

"It's clever. It's not some brutish protective charm designed to kill everything on sight, it operates with rules. And if it's clever then that means that it contains some rudimentary intelligence, and if that's true," and here Grefno waved his fingers in front of his face. "If that's true then that means it can be lied to."

"How? How do we lie to a spell?" said Krillan.

Grefno drew a circle in the air around the group of men. It was suddenly bright daylight and blues skies over them.

"I can make it think that it's yesterday inside this circle. As far as the spell is concerned, it hasn't happened yet. It's still yesterday and it hasn't been used."

"That's clever," said Krillan.

"Yes," said Grefno. "It is."

"Is it time travel? Is it somehow yesterday in here?"

"No, of course it isn't. That would be ridiculous, you know that. However, the heat barrier doesn't know it. It thinks it can't possibly hurt us in here because it hasn't happened as yet."

With a few nervous glances at each other, Krillan and the men followed Grefno through the gap in the heat barrier and towards the village. There was no sign of the creature as the men advanced, weapons at the ready.

"Captain Krillan!" A shout came from a building, and a figure came running out. To everyone's surprise, the figure threw her arms around the captain and hugged him. "I'm so happy to see you alive! And to think, only yesterday I thought you were a total prick!"

The Captain looked back abashed, red faced in front

of the other soldiers. "How kind, Miss Carleaf," he said at last.

"We need to get to a place of safety," said Grefno. "Is the shelter open?"

Private Shaule came jogging up behind Leah. "I would have recommended the Inn," he said. "But unfortunately it has been compromised. Nowhere is safe I'm afraid."

Sergeant Wallas lowered his weapon and nodded to the two militiamen to do likewise. "Honoured Sage, what's happening?"

"I don't know!" said Niaal, wide eyed. "My magic isn't working! There's something wrong, something blocking it. I have been trapped in my room all this time." Niaal followed the men out of the room, along the corridor.

"Captain Krillan has found the Sage Grefno. They believe they have found the cause of the sickness."

"Grefno still lives? Oh, this is wonderful news. I feared everyone to be dead."

"Who is guarding the Mage?" said Wallas.

"The Castle guards have sealed the inner sanctum. There's no way anyone can get in or out. I tried to make contact, but there is no one to be found who would answer me." Niaal looked down at the dead bodies. "Tell me, how much has Captain Krillan found out?"

"Hard to say sir," Wallas said, reloading his weapon. "We know that the sickness is more complicated than we first thought. It may well have spread to other Mages across Inan."

"I see. This is dreadful. Dreadful! Has anyone been in contact with General Vale yet? Has anyone alerted him?"

"Not as far as I'd know, Sir. Besides, all transports have left for the front. There's no way we can get a message in or out."

Niaal twisted his cloak, nervously. "Come," he said. "It's not safe here."

With a squawk of static, Wallas' comm burst into life

"Wallas? You receiving me?" It was Krillan's voice. "Please report your position."

"Captain Krillan? Sergeant Wallas here, receiving you loud and clear, Sir. We're in the Castle, moving towards the postern gate."

"Sergeant! What news?" said Grefno said, cutting in. "Any survivors? Anyone at all?"

"Not looking good, sir. Looks like the worm's handiwork again. Only one person found alive so far."

"It's better than nothing. Who is it?"

"The Sage Niaal, Sir. Only one still alive."

There was silence.

"Captain? You still with me, sir?"

"Yes.... I mean, yes, Sergeant. We're in the village, planning our next move. Hold your position, please."

In the Castle, Niaal paced impatiently up and down in front of Wallas and his men. "Well? What do they say?"

"They're conferring now, sir. They say we're to hold."

"Tell them to hurry up. That worm could be here any second."

"Very good sir, said Wallas, discreetly flicking the comms switch to transmit. Krillan and the others were now hearing their conversation.

"How long did you say you'd been hiding in here, Sir?"

"What? Oh, since this morning. Since Grefno came back from the town."

"Did you have the chance to talk to him at the time? Did he tell you anything useful? Anything at all?"

"No. No, I didn't even see him."

"And you've been locked in your study all this time?"

"Yes. Really, Sergeant, must I explain everything?"

"But if that's the case... how did you know about the worm?" said Wallas.

Niaal sneered. "Peasant!" he screamed, flicking his fingers. Wallas dived as a sheet of air became as hard as diamond, sharp as steel, killing the other two soldiers flanking him instantly. Wallas dropped to his knees, aiming to fire, but found that he suddenly couldn't move.

Giving up on his weapon, Wallas mentally re-routed the electrical charges in his life support, trying to jumpstart his seized muscles. Niaal came closer, spitting with fury. "You were all dead anyway," he laughed.

Grefno looked at Krillan as they heard Wallas dying. Leah backed away, her hands over her ears.

There was a stunned silence from Krillan as he attempted to take it all in. "But why?"

"It's the plants. It's always been about the plants," Grefno said.

"I don't understand," said Leah. "What's about the plants? "

Grefno looked out towards the Garden, his face full of worry. "Inan has seen all manner of warfare. Biological, mechanical, magical, but never agricultural before. It all started with weeds. They had been struggling to contain an outbreak of weeds; our enemies, I mean. They found a way to destroy them. Not to contain, but to totally and entirely eradicate an entire plant species, using magic. The only trouble is, if they could control one species they could control others too."

"What sort of species?" Leah asked.

"Corn. Barley. Maize. The staple crops. They would have the power to starve a country. Starve the world if need be."

"So what happened? I mean, there haven't been any major famines these last fifteen years, so something must have happened."

"We found a way to stop them," said Grefno. "The Sage Niaal, together with General Vale, or Colonel Vale as he was in those days, helped your father come up with a plan. Our enemies were so wrapped up in magic and science that they forgot about the natural world around them. They were so convinced that they could control the botanical structure of the world, that they forgot just how closely dependant plants and animals are. It's like this: Kill all the bees and the plants won't pollinate. Without pollination, the plants all die, without plants the animals die, and give it six months after that and we all die too."

"They used bees?" said Krillan.

"No. Not bees." Grefno sighed. "Your father and Niaal stopped them controlling the plants. I never had the chance to discuss how with your father, he died too suddenly. Niaal was always very modest about his part in it, putting it down to your father's expertise and brilliance with plants. But he lied. To defeat a botanical weapon, they must have countered with zoological warfare."

Leah looked at him, suddenly understanding. "He found a worm. Didn't he?"

"Yes. A filthy creature normally found burrowing in the Hirvan wastes. An evolutionary blind alley. It has the ability to make plants obey it. It can animate plant life, by some crude form of telekinesis."

"But if it's vegetarian, why the big teeth?" said Leah.

"I never said it was vegetarian. Living in a desert, a creature that size, it has to be able to consume any and every living thing that comes along. It has no natural predators, because its skin is poisonous. Some people say that's why the Hirvan wastes are like they are. That they were green and fruitful before the worms settled there."

"But the Hirvan wastes are on the other side of the world from us," said Krillan. "How would they ever have gotten hold of one?"

"Towards the end of the war, a madman, a lunatic warlord, turned his hand to ever more extreme weapons. For years we thought he might have tried to seed Hirvan worms, but we never found any proof. His own men were left in a vegetative state by his use of them. The warlord died in the chaos that followed the collapse of Varn. Obviously, somehow or other, Niaal must have come across one."

"It would explain a lot," said Leah.

"But they can't all be the result of this one worm?"

"No. What if there are lots of them, though? What if they were scattered all over the world? What if there are groups of people like us, right now, wondering how they're going to sort this out?"

"But why don't their Mages do something?" Krillan said.

Leah looked at him. "You mean like ours did?"

Grefno sank to his knees in shock. "Or what if they're all dead..." He felt his vision narrowing, suddenly ashamed that he might faint. "But if that were so, then what is holding the magic together? What is containing the vast magical energies of Inan?"

"Niaal?" Krillan said.

"He's insane," whispered Grefno. "He deliberately infected the Mage. The worm is magical. If a Mage was infected, then perhaps they could spread the illness via magic itself?"

"So how do we stop it?"

"We can't. The Mage is dead. The worm killed him. If we are right, then Niaal has assumed the magical power of the most powerful beings on all of Inan. There is only one solution, only one way to stop him."

"Which is?"

"We kill him, outright. The only trouble is, if we do that without replacing him with another Mage, or rather another set of Mages, then we risk putting an end to magic itself."

"Don't be ridiculous! You might as well say you'll put an end to gravity, or electricity!" said Krillan.

"It's the most powerful piece of magic that the Mages could come up with. Brought in during the treaty that ended the war, it guarantees that no one person can assume total power. And yes, I know that's exactly what he's done! He was instrumental in helping draft the proposals for the spell. This was probably his plan all along." Grefno stared up at the Castle, his face grim. "But the facts remain, if we don't replace him, then the entire magical flow of the world of Inan will almost certainly dissipate and vanish."

"Then we find some new Mages, " said Leah.

"At such short notice? Who do you suggest, Leah? Me? You? Captain Krillan, over there?"

"But, destroying the magic? It's just..." Leah struggled for the words. "It's just wrong."

"This worm? It killed the other Mages?" Krillan said.

"Yes," said Grefno. "It channels magical energy."

"Fine. So in order to take out Niaal, we need to hit him with the same poison."

"You mean we need to go looking for the worm again?" said Leah.

"Oh. Goody," said Rendolph with a complete lack of enthusiasm.

"Not all of us," said Krillan. "Niaal has manipulated events, played us for fools to such an extent that our armed forces, who might have reasonably attempted to stop him, will attack our neighbours in a few hours time. He's making sure that the countries of Allesh and Prash-Romari are in such a state of chaos that there is no-one in a position to oppose him. If the attack goes ahead, then things will escalate quickly, especially if the Mages are not involved, and before long we will have a world at war again. We need to stop the attack. Someone needs to go and tell the general to call it off, tell him that the true enemy is here, back in the Castle."

"I'll go," said Krillan. "Something of this magnitude, he needs to hear it from another officer."

"With the greatest respect," said Grefno, "I think it better if you stay with us." He closed his eyes, and slid a small wooden stick into his wrist-port and withdrew it again. "There. That should tell the good General everything he needs to know. Make sure it goes to him in person. If Niaal has set himself up as some kind of super-Mage, then he'll be blocking every transmission as it is. It must be delivered in person."

"Fine, but who do we send?" said Krillan.

"Rendolph, there's no easy way around this." said Leah. "Thing is, and I say this as a friend, you're going to be pretty hopeless for what's coming next. You can't shoot, you're a bit of a coward, and are probably the least intelligent person currently left alive in the village." She smiled at him. "Which is why I'm volunteering you."

"No."

"Yes."

"I'm not leaving you."

"Yes you are. You want to save Gim, to save all of us? Well that's what I'm telling you to do."

Leah handed Rendolph the datastick from Grefno.

"This message? You need to take care of it," said Grefno. "The first part is a letter of authorisation. The second is personal to General Vale, from me. Without this, Vale will launch us into a war that will threaten to spill out and destroy all of us. Rendolph, if you fail to get this message to Vale then Niaal will have won. Everything we've achieved since the Great War will have been for nothing."

Rendolph held the stick in his hand tightly, his knuckles white. "How do I get it to him?"

"There's one machine left that everyone has forgotten about," said Krillan, smiling at Leah. "I think it's time I paid a visit to our friends the firemen. They can take him as far as the next town where he can pick up a fast military transport."

Leah beamed. "Oh! Lovely." She smiled at Krillan as he ran in the direction of the fire station, calling after him. "Did you ever consider a career in the fire service, Captain? I think the uniform would suit you."

One of Krillan's men came running from the opposite direction. He stood to attention before Grefno.

"Sir, the worm is on the move again. It's heading this way, we need to get out if we're going. We've built a barricade across the street, but I don't know if it's enough to hold it for long."

"Thank you, private." Grefno turned to Rendolph again. "Niall may try and kill you. There is every possibility that he will succeed."

Leah and Rendolph looked at each other, sadly.

"Oh, Leah. I only every wanted to be a Gardener."

"Me too. Will you go?"

"You know I will."

She smiled. "Is there anything I can do for you before you go? I mean, anything I can do for you apart from showing you my boobies?" she said.

He smiled. "No. That would have been it," he said, laughing.

She smiled at him again, shaking her head. "Pervert."

"Sir, it's overrun the barricades! We're pulling back from the high street. We have to go now!"

The army had set fire to some of the buildings in the village in an attempt to create a firebreak against the worm. There were people running down the streets carrying what weapons they could find. Looking towards the market Leah felt a sudden pang of fear as she saw her own house burst into flames. Every single memory of her parents associated with it, now burning. The air was heavy with the smoke from thatched roofs.

With a crash of sparks the barricade collapsed, and Leah saw the worm once more. It seemed bigger than it had in the tunnels, and at first she wondered if it might be some new beast. But the markings were too distinct, too regular.

"Run for it!" yelled a soldier as Rendolph and Leah sped down the street after the fleeing crowd. Turning back, Leah saw the man raise his weapon to fire at the beast, but he was too slow. Like lightning the tail of the creature snaked through the air, punching the man in the chest. His armour held, but he was winded. Turning to run back, Leah saw him look at her and shake his head.

Understanding, she grabbed Rendolph and threw herself to the floor as the solider ignited the thermal grenade he had been holding. The creature screamed in anger and reared to its full height, shaking its head to adjust its vision after the sudden flare. Leah grabbed Rendolph's arm and dragged him down the street after her.

The firemen were waiting for them, their aircraft ready to go. It was a small ship, built for speed, with a crew of two anxious looking pilots.

"You ready?" shouted Leah to the pilots above the noise of the engines. They nodded and gave the thumbs up. "Take this man, and get him as near to the front as you can. Don't stop for anything or anyone."

"Who is he?" one of the pilots shouted. "Some kind of secret agent?"

"He's a composting assistant," said Leah, smiling at her friend. "Third class."

Rendolph felt a lurch in his stomach as the aircraft lifted off. He saw the worried face of his friend one last time, before she turned to face the creature.

The barricade collapsed as, with a hideous squeal of triumph, the worm pulled itself into the street. Rendolph could see Shaule and Krillan fire their weapons at it, saw Grefno and Leah running towards the inn, and then they were gone as he was pulled up in to the clouds.

CHAPTER ELEVEN

Rendolph was used to heights, working as he did in the Garden. He loved the Garden and his job there, and in truth enjoyed being able to take himself away from people, up into the branches of the trees. He had been known to harness up in the morning, and then spend all day up in the canopy. However, as accustomed to heights as he was, he was utterly unprepared for the journey by air.

For starters it was cold. No one had warned him of this, and he was glad of the fur-lined jacket, gloves and leather helmet he had been given by the pilots.

They were above the clouds. It was a sight that Rendolph had never imagined he would get to see in his lifetime. He had been in clouds before, but never above them. Once, during a heavy and oppressive summer storm, the clouds had come down so low that, working as he did in the highest branches of the tallest redwoods, he had vanished from the view of those below. The cloud had been grey and wet. Nothing like the brilliant soft white mountains spread out below him.

The aircraft was small and fast, and made Rendolph think of a stretched soap bubble, the way that the light caused colours to skip across its thin skin. At first he had held on tightly to the seatbelt that held him in place, but he soon fell into a sense of ease as the craft skipped and bobbed its way through the atmosphere.

Rendolph looked below, and through the gaps in the clouds he could see fields, meadows, whole towns and villages. He saw the shadow of a cloud moving across what must be the great plain of Waddon, marvelling at the fact that he was able to see such a thing so many thousands of feet up in the air He looked down, delighting in the sheer beauty of it all.

He screwed his eyes up in confusion. There was no cloud below him there. The sun was behind him. Indeed, he could feel the warmth on his back through the film of the aircraft. There should be a cloud causing the shadow below, and yet there was none there.

But that was absurd. How could a shadow be creeping across the ground at such speed if there were no cloud to cause it?

He tried to attract the attention of the pilots, but they waved him away, deeply involved in their navigation. When at last they had finished what they were doing and were ready to speak to him, the gap in the clouds had closed, leaving Rendolph none the wiser to what he had witnessed.

The Waddon plain was a large fertile area of arable farmland. Small towns and villages pockmarked its broad expanse, following the course of the half dozen or so rivers that watered the rich soil. It was the breadbasket of the north.

The gorse swept across it in a single afternoon. Three-meter high bushes with thorns the size of bayonets, the plants grew and spread like water poured on a marble floor. Trapped in their homes, people watched as the light was blotted out around them, the windows going dark. Those unlucky enough to be caught out of doors were killed outright, speared by the razor sharp spines on the branches of the plants. Herds of cattle were driven in front of the swathe in terror, until they either fell into the rivers and drowned, or else were forced to stop by the sheer weight of bodies piled upon the electric fences that divided the landscape into farms.

In three short hours, the gentle, lush landscape was transformed into a thorny, spiky green hell. From his vantage point in their air, it had been the growth of the bushes that Rendolph had seen, mistaking it for the shadow of a cloud.

They put down some thirty miles to the north, landing on a stretch of open road. The highway was already full of soldiers heading for the Prash-Romari border in orderly lines. No aircraft would be able to fly any nearer than this, unless on operational missions, and so this was as far as the firemen could take Rendolph before they ran the risk of being shot down as a potentially hostile aircraft.

Hitching a lift on a fuel tanker, he settled himself down to a rattling, bumpy ride.

He passed columns of men in black armour, heading for the front. The occasional purples, reds and yellows of mission specialists and Chemical Warriors stood out like flowers in a coalfield. At every stage Rendolph was stopped and questioned as to who he was, but the authorisation from Grefno seemed to carry more weight than any obstacle thrown in his way. And so it was he finally came to the front.

The war had not yet started but even he could see that it was only a matter of time. Siege engines and tanks had been brought up from the rear. Grey uniformed artificers were busy laying wires and cables.

He had no real idea of where the General might be, and it seemed that the military were in no real hurry to find him, either, despite how impressive his letter of authorisation was. He found that he was desperate for sleep, and having made his request clear to the most senior officer he could find, he crawled away into a supply tent to sleep, before he collapsed with exhaustion.

Eventually a portly officer woke him by shining a torch in his face. "We've got some good news for you, farm boy. We've found the General for you!"

"Oh good," said Rendolph, with rather less gratitude than he might have shown. "Is he outside?"

The officer smiled. "No chance. He's way up line. Have you ever been in a forward position before?"

"I've never been anywhere before."

"It could get a bit dangerous up there, so I looked around in stores and we've got some kit left that you can use. No idea how long it's been sitting around." He emptied the contents of a bag out onto a table in the tent. "That's the army for you. We hold onto things until we're ordered to let go of them. Hope it fits. It's a bit out of date in most respects, but should see you safer than what you're wearing now."

It was a suit of plastic armour. Green in colour, with pouches and pockets all down the front. Rendolph knew what it was straight away.

"This is a Gardener's armour, isn't it?"

"That's right. Quite rare it is too. There were only a few of your lot here and there, no more than a dozen in the whole army. Experts in camouflage and dangerous plants, that sort of thing. Most of that kind of work gets done by Chemical Warriors these days, but technically you're still entitled to wear it. It won't stop a direct hit, but it might deflect it enough to do less damage. It's loaded to protect you against chemical and biological attack, and saturated in chemicals to provide defences against psychological and hypnotic weapons."

Rendolph remembered seeing pictures of army Gardeners when he was a boy. There was one on the wall of the office back in the Garden; Leah's dad, it was.

"Right then. I'll leave you to get kitted up. I've arranged a personnel carrier to pick you up. It'll zip you over to where the general is in no time." The officer smiled again, leaving Rendolph alone.

He began to pull on the armour, marvelling at how light it felt once on. He didn't feel like a soldier, but he looked like one now. The armour was old, but outwardly it looked pretty much the same as everyone else's. Once kitted out, Rendolph exited the tent, noticing the stares of other soldiers drawn to his archaic get-up

"Ah, it fits I see. Well, that's a good start, anyway. Have you brought everything with you need?" The officer said.

"Yes. I mean, I think so. Never done this before."

"You'll be fine. Stick with the lads and they'll cover you if it gets nasty. Has anyone given you a sword yet?"

Rendolph shook his head. "We don't use them in the Garden. No need for them."

"I see. Hang on then." The officer ducked inside a tent and re-emerged a few seconds later. "Here you go," he said, handing Rendolph a machete. "More your thing I'd have thought. You've used one before, I imagine?"

"Only on plants."

"Well, who knows what you'll find out there, eh? Here take this while you're at it." He handed Rendolph a belt, with a scabbard to take the blade. "Don't I get a blaster or something?"

"Not unless you can provide me with the appropriate qualifications proving you've had the correct training and won't shoot one of my men in the back by accident. But honestly, I don't think you'll need one. Just do what the boys tell you and if anyone starts shooting, run as fast as you can. Come on, I'll see if I can find you that transport. It's probably better if we get you there and back again before anything major goes off."

Rendolph's face fell. "Thanks," he said, his voice devoid of all enthusiasm. "That'd be wonderful."

"Here," said Grefno. "Help me undress."

"Really?" Leah looked at him, confused. "Look, time and a place for everything, right? I mean the age difference alone is a hurdle."

"Stop trying to lighten this with humour. Help me get my armour off."

Leah helped him with the straps holding his shoulder pads on. "Well I thought it was funny," she said. "Come on Krillan, give me a hand."

Grefno and Leah had taken refuge in one of the shops that overlooked the market square. When the worm had attacked, they had found a place to hide while the soldiers managed to fend the beast off with their weaponry. Once the coast was clear, Krillan had come to find them. Together they managed to get the Sage out of his yellow armour and the tight fitting bodysuit. "You need to put this on," Grefno said, handing the armour to Leah.

"Er... why?"

"Because it will keep you alive. Now do it."

"And what will keep you alive?"

"Captain Krillan will. Now do it. Please, Leah."

Leah looked to Krillan for advice.

"Do as he says," said Krillan. "I'd give you mine gladly, but I need it to stay in contact with the troops. Suits have very short range capability that has nothing to do with magic. Works on simple radio waves."

Leah had never worn armour before. The sensation was

not unpleasant, and she was surprised at the way she enjoyed the feeling of the tiny fibres burrowing down into her nerves. The helmet and shoulder pads fitted easily enough, but the rest of it clacked and jangled and got in the way. She was just the wrong size and shape for it.

"Wasn't built for people with hips, Grefno."

"It will have to do. If the worm attacks, if it stings you, the suit will fire off charges to defend you. In battle it's designed to keep you alive long enough to be airlifted out." Grefno rubbed his chin, worriedly. "Of course, it's a Chemical Warrior's suit so it does a whole raft of things that the usual armour doesn't. Probably best if you don't mess with it, just in case."

There came a cry from the street. It was Shaule. "Captain Krillan! We've got another sighting of the creature. It's heading towards us!"

"Here we go again," said Krillan. "I'm on my way!"

The worm was now at the far end of town. Looking back, Leah saw it flick out its tail, sending militiamen flying through the air. She saw another squad of militia guards try to assemble a small cannon, but the creature moved with incredible speed before they could bring the weapon to bear.

"So now what?" Leah said.

Grefno's face fell. "I don't know. I was trying to research this thing when it all went wrong in the Castle. And now I can't even contact one of the other Sages to find out, assuming they're still alive, of course."

"Find out what?"

"How to kill it. This creature can be killed, Leah. We

need only understand how. If it has a relationship with plants, presumably there is one key trigger that will prove fatal to it."

Leah looked puzzled. "But why?" she said. "Why should there be? Not wanting to sound pessimistic or anything here, but really, why?"

"It's how that kind of magic works. The creature will have power to influence plants because it itself is vulnerable, on a magical level, to one in particular. If Captain Krillan and his men kill it, its hold over the plants will be broken."

"But even if we do, the other Mages will still be dead. What will stop us from falling back into barbarism?"

The Sage smiled. "Science."

"Science? Science will save us?"

"No more monsters and angels, no more wizards and demons. Just people. Clever people using their brains." Grefno looked at the market square. The worm had disappeared again. "All gone quiet," he said. "Good. We need to find a way back into the Castle so we can find the strain of plant that kills the ugly brute. If only I could remember it. It was one of the common flowers. One of the Meadowsweet variety. If only I could remember which one though..."

"Polythryantium michconis," Leah said.

Grefno turned to her in amazement. "What?"

"When Gim and I were in the tunnels we saw it growing there. We wondered at the time how it got there. Whoever brought the worm these must have put it there to keep the beast at bay. It wouldn't go near the stuff."

Grefno threw his arms around Leah. "You really should have mentioned this before! Well done, child!" He ran down the road, beckoning her to follow. "Come on! We need to find the captain!"

Grefno and Leah ran across the market square, suddenly on fire with hope.

"Krillan!" bellowed Grefno.

"Krillan, we need you!" Leah turned to look up the high street towards the Inn when she felt Grefno's hand tighten its grip.

"No..."

She glanced back. The worm was directly in front of them.

"We really need that plant," said Grefno.

"But only I know where to find it!" said Leah.

"I know. Steady yourself, we have to move quickly. Back away very slowly."

The creature swayed from side to side, its vile tongue tasting the air as it decided which victim to go for first.

"Run!" Grefno shouted and Leah ran, heading for the doorway of one of the houses in front of her. She turned as she heard a scream, and saw Grefno on his back, pinned down by the beast.

"No!" screamed Leah, running back towards him.

"Keep back!" Grefno yelled, drawing a circle in the air with his fingers. The circle took the shape of a blazing ring of fire, and the creature recoiled as if stung, but Grefno was still pinned down. Turning to face her, the worm hissed angrily. Leah ran, ran faster than she had in her life, as fast as she would have run to her fathers arms if he were to return at that very moment.

She ran to the well, and without a second's hesitation grabbed the rope and slid down as fast as she dared, her armoured gloves shielding her against rope burn.

"No!" Grefno shouted. "Not on your own!" But it was too late, she had gone. Grefno flicked his fingers and darts of glass appeared in front of him, finding weak points in the worm's belly and forcing it to leave hold of him. The creature backed off as Grefno pulled himself to his feet. He was breathing hard and he was sure the worm had broken one of his ribs. His leg felt numb from being crushed by the beast.

The worm turned to look at him once more, blinked twice and then slid slowly across the square. Towards the well.

"Oh no you don't!" Grefno said, hobbling after it. He conjured poison gas out of thin air with one hand, raising the temperature of the stones on the ground to boiling point with the other, but the beast only made it to the well all the more speedily.

As Grefno summoned his strength for one last attack, the creature flicked its tail, sending him crashing to the ground. He landed badly and did not move again.

Satisfied, the creature reared up to its full height, took one last look around the market square, and then slithered over the wall and into the well, following Leah down into the darkness.

CHAPTER TWELVE

Across the face of Inan, on every continent, magic, the stabilising factor in the culture of a whole world, began to buckle and shift. Imaginary creatures battled in the sky while the computers on board fighter aircraft wrestled with entirely imaginary numbers that were attempting to bring them down. Sea monsters swarmed ashore in ever greater numbers. Ordinary people briefly developed superhuman powers, and then lost them again as suddenly. Terrified and looking for blame, neighbour accused neighbour and country accused country.

On the Allesh/Prash-Romari border, General Vale gazed down on the great plain that lay ahead of him.

There had been no word from the Castle. This was only to be expected. To ensure the surprise of the attack, all comms had been silenced. The Sage Niaal had overseen this directly, giving it his personal attention.

In a few short hours time Vale would give the signal to attack, the magical artificers would raise the protective screen that had hidden the army from prying eyes and they would swarm down across the border into neighbouring land.

But what would they find when they got there?

As soon as she reached the bottom of the well, Leah started running, still unaccustomed to the feel of the armour she was wearing. The helmet allowed her to see in the dark, which was an unexpected bonus. She found she could also pick up trails and traces through the visor of the helmet. Some, she quickly realised, were infrared, other were indicators showing directions of airflow, chemical make up of the atmosphere, and electrical activity.

Leah was also delighted to find that that as she ran, the suit helped her. She was much faster than she would normally be, more agile. Which made her wonder if she was stronger too?

Following the tunnels, Leah easily made her way towards where she and Rendolph had seen the Meadowsweet roots. Covering ground far quicker than they had before, Leah stopped, appalled to find herself facing a rock fall. The tunnel had collapsed, blocking her way completely. Leah wracked her brains, trying to remember if there was another way, if they had seen another tunnel on their journey, and as she did so she was amazed to see a map of the tunnel system suddenly displayed on the inside of the visor. It showed the route she had just taken in red. In green was a map of what she supposed must be the entire tunnel system, taken from her memory.

"That's clever," she said, to no one. "Trouble is, how accurate is my memory?"

The red line of the path she had travelled was accurate, as the armour had worked out her position to an inch. She could see where the red and green paths diverged in places, however, where her memory had let her down.

The green map showed another tunnel leading off from the one she had travelled along. She retraced her steps carefully and found that there was indeed another path. Presumably it was one of the routes the worm took in order to avoid the Meadowsweet roots. Looking behind her for any sign of danger, she set off down the path, following the green bouncing line in front of her. The Meadowsweet wasn't far. All she needed to do now was find it, and bring it back to Grefno, if he was still alive.

The suit emitted beeps and clicks as she went, presumably feeding her information, but Leah could only guess as to what it all meant. There were no bright red signs saying 'DANGER!' so she assumed it was safe to continue.

Soon she ran through some chambers and caverns that she remembered passing with Rendolph. The roots of the Meadowsweet weren't far now. Of course, how she was going to get it out again was another matter entirely.

Turning left, Leah crossed a small patch of wet ground. The visor started to display so much information that Leah found it difficult to see where she was going. She tried making the information go away, but had to give up, raising the visor and looking out with her own eyes. Of course, once the helmet was off, she could see nothing at all, being suddenly plunged into pitch black darkness. "Could really use a torch here," she said aloud.

At once the suit punched out a powerful light, illuminating the tunnel.

"Ah. That's good. Thank you, suit." Leah crouched low to look at the water. "Voice activated, eh? Well if you're listening, I could really use half a dozen bronzed fire-fighters right now." She looked around the cave, warily. "Oh well. Can't win them all.

Suddenly, the suit rippled, causing Leah's muscles to tighten and her heart to beat faster. With a shock, she realised that it had very slightly upped her adrenaline levels. Slipping her helmet back on she saw a large bright red sign saying 'Danger!'

"Right then. Thanks, suit," said Leah. The green map had been over written with a red path as she had made her way along it. A yellow dot showed her position. A red dot was making its way slowly towards her, from the way she had just come. It was to this that the danger sign was attributed.

"Time to go!" Leah ran, following the tunnel round to where the Meadowsweet had been.

The Meadowsweet roots were poking down from the dry earth ceiling, and it took Leah a mere matter of seconds to collect a large enough sample for synthesis. "I need somewhere to keep this," said Leah to the suit. At once a flap opened on the shoulder section, and a small black cylinder fell out. "Thanks."

The end of the cylinder unscrewed, and Leah found to her joy that it was just big enough to hold a fairly decent sized sample of roots. Resealing the cylinder, Leah noticed a button on its side. She pressed it and, with a snap, the cylinder extended into a spear, its head crackling with an electric charge.

With one eye on the steadily approaching yellow dot of the worm, Leah headed up the tunnel. She needed to get back to the surface before the beast caught up with her.

In the darkness of the Mage's inner sanctum, the hideous thing that had once been the Mage writhed and slopped against the glistening membrane of the egg sac.

Soon it would feed.

It snaked its thoughts out across the face of the planet, drawing in its brethren, the skinless, eyeless creatures that had once gone by the name of Mage, but were now no more than beasts. Worms.

They embraced each other through the magical conduits that surrounded the world of Inan, revelling in the rage and destruction that had been unleashed though their manipulation. In every nation, in every city-state or empire across the vast span of the two great continents, the things that had once been the Mages, the magical giants of the world of Inan, finally withdrew and succumbed to the magical infection that had been plaguing them the past months. Bad things happened in ever-greater numbers.

One by one, the Mage's physical shapes bloomed and blossomed under the weight of the sickness. Joined to one mind, they sat in their towers, their laboratories and temples, and waited for the feast to begin.

Leah carried on up the corridor, all too aware of the worm, which was now gaining on her. She had found several more rock falls, making her veer away from the routes that would take her back to Grefno and Krillan and the open air. Instead she was being forced deeper and deeper underground, away from her friends and safety.

It was one thing for her to have the Meadowsweet in her hand, but it was another entirely getting it to Grefno.

Leah emerged into the large cavern where she and Gim had been trapped by the vortex previously. Quickly she ran to the trapdoor and found that opening it with the suit on was a great deal easier. The chamber below was now dry, the water levels having receded. Leah crossed to the edge and climbed the ladder set into the wall. The map on her visor said she would find a staircase that would lead up to the Castle if she kept going. What she would do there, she didn't know, but it seemed a better option than facing the worm.

In the village, Grefno was sitting, propped against the wall of one of the shops, drinking bottled water. Krillan came across the market place, rifle in hand.

"You were lucky," he said. "I thought the worm would finish you for good."

Grefno smiled back at the Captain. "Me too. I think I popped a rib, though."

"You should get to the hospital and have it looked at."

Grefno pulled himself to his feet, wincing slightly. "Alright, I promise if we survive this and save the world, I'll get checked out by a doctor."

Krillan and Grefno turned and surveyed their ragtag army. The brown clad militia had been joined by one or two blue uniformed guards, who had managed to escape the slaughter in the Castle. A party of burly farmers, armed with hunting pieces had also joined them, together with some of the braver villagers.

"We have a chance to stop this!" Grefno shouted to the assembled crowd. "We have a chance to stop this tonight. Leah Carleaf, one of the only surviving Gardeners, has gone down into the caves that run beneath the town to find a certain herb that we can use to destroy the worm. We need to make sure she gets it out in one piece. To that end we need men to go down after her." There was a murmur of dissent. "I'm not expecting any of you to engage the worm. Just find Leah, and bring her and the herb back with you." He paused. "At the same time, I need another group to come to the Castle with me. We have unfinished business there that will bring an end to the chaos that currently engulfs us. Captain Krillan, take ten men and go down the well. The rest of you follow me!"

The group split into two,

With a nod to Krillan, Grefno and his troop set off up the hill towards the Castle as Krillan led his men to the lip of the well.

The officer who greeted Rendolph seemed tired and harried. Around him, men were rushing into forward positions.

"So, you're Rendolph? I believe you have a message for the General?"

"Yes, it's most urgent."

The officer touched his wrist-port and an image appeared in the air in-front of Rendolph. It was General Vale.

"Good evening, Gardener Rendolph. You will appreciate that time is short, so please keep what you have to say to a bare minimum. I believe you have suffered no small inconvenience to get here, so I will give you five minutes."

"Right," said Rendolph. "Grefno sent me to give you this," he said, holding up the wooden data stick. "It will tell you everything you need to know."

"We have no way of safely transmitting the data, and it will take you another two hours to reach me on foot. Plug the stick into your own wrist-port and tell me what it says."

Rendolph slid the wooden rod into his wrist-port and at once felt Grefno's thoughts around him. Calm, ordered, peaceful. Rendolph closed his eyes for a second and then spoke. "There's a worm. A Hirvan beast. It's responsible for the sickness. It's been in the water supply and is responsible for making us sick." He saw the General tense in front of him, suddenly paying him more attention.

"To whom am I speaking?" said the general. "Is that you, old friend?"

Rendolph felt Grefno's thoughts inside of him, forcing a smile that he knew was not his.

"It's a bit hard to understand, really. It seems he's sort of planted his personality into this data stick. I think he wants you to be absolutely certain of what he's asking you to do here." Rendolph said. "He really is worried about this worm thing."

"Then why doesn't he have it killed?"

"We're working on it. The thing is, the sickness has affected the Mage. Grefno says one of the Sages, Niaal, has found a way to attack the Mage, and has probably killed him."

The General stiffened at this, though he made no reply. Rendolph continued. "He says that all the Mages in Inan are linked together somehow. Some suicide pact that apparently exists to make sure that if one attacks the other they all go the same way. He says it was supposed to make the world a safer place, but it has done the exact opposite." Rendolph stopped, wondering how this was going down with the General. "Because the Mages are all joined to each other in some magical way, by making one of them sick, he's infected the rest. So magic's gone all screwy. All over the planet. Niaal hopes to use the confusion to rule the world. It's all part of his plan, all part of his scheme. The war is a diversion. He says it's given you a reason to go away and fight, and in doing so leave the Castle open to attack from within. You have to call off the attack and return to the Castle at once. Our neighbours are not our biggest problem, aggressive and nasty though they might be. You're to call off the attack and return to the Castle at once, as quick as you can."

"Colonel?"

The officer with Rendolph snapped to attention.

"Sir?"

"Code blue. Repeat code blue. We're calling off the attack. The protective screen to remain in place, all units to withdraw, effective immediately. Contact air support and tell them we need the ten fastest ships they have and we need them immediately." He turned to face Rendolph. "Gardener Rendolph? You will consider yourself under my command. Let's see if we can't get you to earn that armour." He turned to one of the officers in his headquarters. "Have a squad of assault commandos fully tooled up and ready to take off as soon as the aircraft touch down. Light weapons, going for speed and agility over firepower. We have a long night ahead of us, gentlemen."

Leah was lost. According to the data projected onto the inside of her visor, she should be standing inside the Castle. In fact she should be in the energy vent that led directly up to the Mage's chamber. Instead she was in a cold, damp place, the walls wet with brown slime. Instead of the blue pulsating mass of light she was expecting to see, there was nothing except a sickly green glow and water lapping at the lower end of the chamber.

All three versions of the maps currently were in broad agreement with each other. It was just that they were so obviously wrong.

She was halfway across the chamber when in the gloom in front of her she saw the unmistakable shape of the worm. Catching sight of Leah it sprung up, tensing itself ready to leap towards her. Without waiting for any further encouragement, Leah started to run. Lights flashed and blinked inside her armour, but she had no time to pay them attention even if she'd known what they meant.

"Help me, suit!" she called, and at once she felt her

limbs being aided by the armour. The worm hissed its rage and then began sliding after her.

The floor of the chamber was wet, and gently sloped downwards as she crossed it, meaning that she was soon knee deep in water. With a final beep, the lights on her suit flashed a bright red and went dead. She panicked, realising that it was almost impossible to move her limbs.

"Marvellous. That was the battery warning light, I take it?"

Leah began unbuckling her armour, pulling off her greaves and chest plate as she waded through the water.

She looked around the chamber; the beauty of the Mage's quarters was something she had only ever seen in books. If this was indeed the Mage's chamber she had entered, then it was heartbreaking to see it defiled in this way.

With a deafening roar, the worm rose up behind her, crashing its way through the chamber. Leah waded through the water trying to get to the door on the far side before it did, hoping that she would still have a chance of escape. But the worm was too fast.

Leah stood, holding the spear in front of her, with no clear idea of what to do next.

"Right. I've got a spear. I've got a spear packed full of Meadowsweet. I've got a spear packed full of Meadowsweet, which I think is fatal to worms. Now what?"

To her enormous delight, the spear gave a small beep. "Separate battery pack?" The spear beeped again. "Oh, I love you, spear. Now, what do I do with it?"

"Keep very still," said a voice, from behind her. "It's deciding what to do next. You have something that worries it, or else it would have attacked."

"Who's there?"

"You're safe, as long as you do as I say. I'm one of the Sages. My name is Niaal."

Niaal! Thoughts of Wallas flashed before her eyes. Dead because of him. Her mother close to death, all because of him. Rendolph, the people in the village, all because of him. Rage pulsed through her like an angry red tide, filling her with the urge to kill him.

"Honoured Sage?" Leah said, her voice trembling with fear. "Please help me!"

"It's alright, child," said Niaal, coming closer. "It's Leah, isn't it? Leah Carleaf? One of our Gardeners. Wherever did you come by that armour you just discarded by the way?"

"I... I took it from the body of another Sage. Grefno. I found him dead outside and hoped the armour would save me," she lied.

"Good thinking," smiled Niaal. "Grefno dead, eh? Well that's a turn up."

Niaal stepped around Leah, never once taking his eyes off the worm.

"Why doesn't it attack, Leah? What have you got that is making it so hesitant?

Normally these things will kill on sight. So what makes you so special?" He swept his hands over the spear. "Ah. Meadowsweet. You have been doing your homework, haven't you?" Niaal stepped back. "It can smell the Meadowsweet and is scared of it.

"Yes. Grefno told me it would kill the worm. He said I was to find a Sage and give the Meadowsweet to him. He said they'd know what to do with it."

"Thought so." Niaal kicked her in the small of the back, sending her flying. "Liar! Grefno's as alive as you are! I'd have known if he died."

Leah span round, pointing the spear at Niaal.

"That won't work on me, child. It only kills worms."

"You mean this stuff actually works?" Leah beamed. "Thank you, Niaal. That's wonderful news!"

The worm hovered, swaying between the two of them. She pointed the spear at Niaal's heart. "I can still run you though with it though."

"Yes, you could. But then I don't think there's any real chance of that happening, do you?" Niaal spread his fingers and Leah felt herself pushed down to the floor. "I'm no ordinary Sage, you stupid child. Not some half-wit like poor old Grefno, but a fully empowered Magus, filled with the magical tides of the entire world. There is nothing I cannot do right now!"

"The Mage! He'll stop you!" shouted Leah, still trying to conceal from Niaal how much of the truth she knew, hoping it would give her some meagre advantage.

"The Mage? Oh, you poor sweet girl. You think he'll stop me?" Niaal laughed. "I take it you feel very close to your Mage in times of trouble, do you? Well, so you should!" Niaal clicked his fingers and the room was suddenly illuminated by a fiery blue light. "You're standing in him!"

Leah saw that what she had taken to be water was a hideous soup, a thick congealed gravy containing pieces of what looked like circuitry.

The worm hissed, weaving slowly this way and that.

"Of course, it wasn't easy. The death throes of the Mages are causing the magical balance of the whole world to go dangerously out of control. It's not just dear old Allesh that has been inconvenienced, you know." Niaal smirked, enjoying having an audience. "Oh yes, there'll be wars, famines, diseases, all over the planet. Magical creatures on the rampage, unreal things rising up and killing anything in their path." He smiled warmly, his hands held out in an open fashion. "The Mages are all dead. All of them. There is now only me, Niaal, in control of the whole world!"

Niaal held his hands up, delighted to at last declare his greatness to another living person. He would reveal himself to the whole world soon enough, but even so, it always played to have a dress rehearsal. "The age of the Mages has come to an end! Behold, the age of the Ultra-Magus! Worm! Kill her!"

With a hideous shriek, the worm opened its slavering jaws and lunged at Leah. One of its vile fangs pierced her shoulder pad and snapped off, spewing foul smelling poison into her that burned as she fell.

With an almost superhuman effort, Leah raised the spear and plunged it into the creature's scaly skin, the battery pack burning itself out as it forced the blade though the tough hide.

"Eject cargo!" Leah shouted. "Now!"

The tiny brain in the spear, the only surviving subset of her yellow armour, pressed the meadowsweet forwards. Up it went, through the hollow steel point and straight into the worm's bloodstream.

Inches from her face, the creature paused, its eyes seeing her with appalling clarity. Then it rose up to its full height, and with a deafening roar came crashing down onto Leah, plunging her world into darkness.

CHAPTER THIRTEEN

Krillan raced through the tunnel, his armour following the scent of the worm and the unmistakable electronic footprint of Leah's own armour. Rounding the corner that led to the great chamber, he unlocked the safety from his weapon.

"Fix bayonets!" he shouted to the regulars. "The rest of you do your best."

He looked upwards. He had never been this far beneath the Castle before. The huge mystical thought engines that powered it should have been alive with energy. They should all be dead by simple fact of being there, and yet they still lived.

The engines were silent, the cavernous chamber still.

"Climb!" he ordered.

Leah pulled herself up. The worm was dead, it huge bulk lying across her legs, trapping her. Niaal, incandescent with rage was standing over her.

"What have you done?"

"I killed your worm, I think. Sorry about that. Do hope you won't take it personally." She grimaced, looking at her shoulder. "Meadowsweet. Utterly lethal to them. I read it in a book. You were using it to keep the worm in the tunnels, stop him making his way up here though the magical engines. Easy, really."

"It makes no difference."

"If you say so." Leah strained, trying to pull her legs out from under the carcass. "In the book it said they came from the Hirvan wastes. Revolting creatures."

Niaal sneered at her in disgust. "The Hirvan worms are amongst the most misunderstood creatures in the world. They have natural magical abilities that are so strong, so wildly powerful, that they destroyed the civilization which discovered them."

Leah looked puzzled. "What civilization? They come from the Hirvan wastes. No one lives there. It's a desert."

"It is now. But once, it was a paradise. Until the wizards starting messing about with the worms, of course." Niaal circled Leah like a hungry pack animal. "The worms have many uses."

"You used it to kill the Mage."

"No! I killed all the Mages!"

"Do you know how many people will have died because of what you've done?" said Leah.

"Hmm? Oh, millions." He gave a gentle self-effacing smirk. "Literally millions."

"So. No Mage. No Mages, plural. Just you. What next?"

"Nothing." Niaal leered towards her. "Just me." Niaal threw his arms wide. "And my pets!"

Leah jumped in shock as the body of the worm burst, and dozens of smaller creatures came writhing over the ground toward her, each of them the length of a snake, although fatter and with sharp clawed limbs. As the creature shifted, however, Leah was able to pull herself free from the dead body of the great worm, and scramble away from it.

"Oh, that's disgusting! Using babies. Whatever next?"

"Don't worry, Miss Carleaf. They'll grow to full size just as soon as they've fed." He smiled, backing away from the creatures. "And see if you can guess what's for supper?"

Leah frantically looked around for the spear, but it was too far away, still buried in the carcass of the great worm.

"Get off me!" she shouted, kicking a worm away with her foot. "Try that again and I'll get my army on you.

You'll see."

"Your army?" Niaal smirked. "And which army would that be?"

"This one!" said Krillan, blasting the worm into pieces. The creatures turned as one and hissed furiously at Krillan, standing there in the doorway with his men.

"Idiots!" hissed Niaal, in disbelief.

Krillan saluted him, mocking. "Honoured Sage. Looks like the little ones are easier to kill than the adults, doesn't it?"

The worms slithered across the floor towards Krillan and his men, and at once they were caught in a stream of fire from the weapons. Those that made it through were set upon by farmers with scythes and axes. Krillan shot two himself before one wrapped itself around the arm that held his weapon. The beast rose up until it was staring at him face to face; it's teeth dripping wet in the sick green light.

"Oh no you don't!" shouted Krillan, plunging his army knife into the creature, but it was too late. Even as it died, the worm bit Krillan on the shoulder, and they fell together.

With a snarl, Niaal gathered his senses and spun in a circle, generating a disc in mid-air, a smooth shape made of magic and thought. Pushing his arms forwards, it moved across the chamber, driving the men back.

Krillan looked up at him through blurry failing eyes, trying even now to draw his sword.

"Come on, Grefno!" Niaal called. "Where are you?"

The room exploded into colour. A bright light, like daylight in summer, the room suddenly glowed with life; sheer vibrant, affirming life.

"This stops now!" shouted Grefno.

Niaal roared at him. "You won't stop me! You can't. You know what it will mean. You're as powerless as the rest of them."

Grefno smiled.

"Yes. I am. And that's why you've already lost." Grefno pulled Leah's spear from the dead worm and raised it over his shoulder as if to throw it.

Niaal laughed.

"I've stolen the power of every Mage on Inan. Join me and I might let you live, Grefno. But kill me now, before I have ascended to god-hood, and you will destroy the magic forever. Do you understand? Without me there will be no more magic, not now, not ever!"

"I know what will happen," Grefno said.

"Then put down the spear."

Grefno hefted the spear, weighing it in his grasp. "The thing about magic, is that once everyone knows how it's done, it's not magic anymore. It's just science." Grefno closed one eye. "And I like science."

He threw the spear with all his might. Niaal screamed in defiance, as the point pierced his heart. With a look of astonishment he fell to his knees.

"You killed him?" Leah said, hopefully.

"Don't be stupid," said Niaal, pulling himself back to his feet. "You think spears can stop me?" He punched his fist forward and three militiamen exploded into red mist. The spear glowed bright red and melted out of his chest.

"Come on then! Let's see what you've got next!"

"I have no magic that will stop you," said Grefno. "You are too powerful, we both know that."

"Surrender, Grefno? I expected more of you."

"No. Not surrender. You see, magic won't stop you. Not now. All I can do is to take away your magic. Take away everyone's magic."

"And how will you do that?"

"The bite of the worm will do it. It killed the Mage, it'll

kill you."

"But the worms are all dead."

"We don't need an actual worm." Grefno said, turning to Leah. "We just need the venom. Don't we, Leah?"

Leah ripped the worm's tooth from where it was still embedded in her shoulder pad and with one swift, sharp movement, plunged it deep in Niaal's back.

A silent scream left his mouth as he fell to his knees. He looked up at Grefno, poison tears falling from his eyes.

"Bastard," he mouthed and then he was gone. And as Niaal, the Ultra Magus, last and only Supreme Mage of all Inan died, so the magic of the world of Inan died with him.

"Come on!" shouted Grefno. "In a few minutes this whole place will come down around our ears! We need to get out!"

"We need a sample of the worm's toxin!" shouted Leah. "We need it to make an antidote."

"The illness is magical, Leah!" said Grefno. "We shouldn't need it!"

"Well I'm taking no chances," said Leah, dropping a piece of the slime coated skin of the beast into a pocket. "It's my mother we're talking about here."

Leah hauled Krillan to his feet. With her on one side and Shaule on the other, they dragged him from the hall. The surviving soldiers moved as fast as they could as the Castle rumbled its death throes. They saw the great main hall collapse in on itself as they passed through the outer gate, and out onto the hill overlooking the village.

"Everyone down!" shouted Grefno.

Behind them, light poured from the Castle, up into the sky. And then there was silence.

The Castle rose a few feet into the air and then crashed to the ground, the magical construct turning to plasma and jelly as a wave of liquid ectoplasmic surf rolled towards them.

"Run!" Grefno shouted. "The Castle's reverting to the basic building blocks of matter. We need to get clear of it!"

The group ran as fast as they could towards the village, as the wave of blue glowing energy rolled inexorably towards them

"The trees!" Leah shouted. "We need to get to the trees! They're the highest point left for miles!"

"There's no time!" said Grefno. "The houses will have to do. Get upstairs; get everyone on to the rooftops!"

Running into a house, Leah and Shaule dragged Krillan up the stairs before climbing out of a back window. Leah pulled Krillan after her, as they watched the wave glide toward them.

"This is it, then. This is how it ends."

"Almost, but not quite!" Grefno yelled. Looking up, Leah saw lights in the sky ahead, bobbing towards them.

"What is it?" Shaule said. "More beasts?"

"No," said Grefno. "It's alright. I think everything is going to be alright."

The spots of light grew bigger, until Leah was able to see that they were Alleshi aircraft. The vehicles swooped down towards the village, dropping a line of bombs which halted the wave of energy as the ground was churned up in front of it.

"It's not enough!" said Leah. "It's still coming."

"It's alright," said Grefno. "Look, they've bought us enough time."

Leah looked at the glowing mass. With a hiss of steam, it melted away to a fine mist.

"No more magic," said Grefno. "It will take a few hours for the effects to spread out, of course. The Castle was vaguely sentient. It just needed reminding that it couldn't exist any longer."

The aircraft lights grew bigger until they took shape, landing in the fields and lanes leading to the town. One landed in the Market Square. Running downstairs, Leah smiled as Rendolph and General Vale climbed down from the ship they had travelled in.

"Did you stop the war?" Grefno said.

"Of course he did," said Rendolph. "Where's your faith?"

The General embraced his old friend, throwing his arms around Grefno's shoulders in a big bear hug.

"Grefno! You have saved us again!"

"I'd gladly take the credit, but we have Miss Carleaf to thank for our salvation."

The General took her hand and shook it. "Thank you, Leah. I'm sure the story will be told in full soon enough."

"Ow!" said a voice behind them. "My shoulder is killing me!" Krillan stood in the square, rubbing his shoulder.

"Not dead then?" said Rendolph.

"The illness was magical in nature," Grefno smiled. "It's gone. All the magic has gone. The chaos will be immense. It's going to make life difficult for a long time. But not impossible."

"The people who got the illness, will they be waking up too?" said Leah, suddenly full of hope.

"Yes, Leah. Your mother, your friend Gim, everyone. There will be sick people waking up all well again all over the hospital. Your mother will be most surprised to see what her daughter has been up to, I'm sure."

"And the magical catastrophes that have been reported, the manifestations all over Inan?" said the general.

"No more magic. Of course, that will be a catastrophe in itself for a while, but we'll get over it."

Grefno turned to face his friends. "For millennia magic and science have woven themselves around each other on Inan, like creepers twining around a tree. Like... serpents." He grimaced. "But no more. Today we are left with science and nothing else. And who knows where that will take us?" He slapped the General on the back. "Come. There is much work to be done."

Leah watched the two older men as they wandered off, starting to make plans for the future. She slipped back, suddenly wanting something familiar, something normal.

"Can I give you a lift to the hospital?" It was Captain Krillan, looking somewhat embarrassed. "I've still got a horse around here somewhere and I know you've got more than one reason to visit the two Doctor Barrots."

"That would be great, Captain," she said, surprised at how suddenly delighted she felt to be asked. There was going to be a lot to re-evaluate in the next few months. Maybe the Captain wasn't as much of a total prick as she had thought, after all.

As the great Castle, the beautiful symbol of the age of magic finally sank away into the clean soil, the group walked towards the hospital, to their friends, and the future.

Whatever that would be.

THE END

Mike Maddox's senses departed him, after being a lifelong fan of the short story, and in a moment of weakness he wrote the script for the *Lion Graphic Bible*, a full-scale comic strip adaptation of the entire Bible. He has no idea what he must have been thinking. Since publication, the book has won an award at the prestigious Angoulême Comics Festival, and has been translated into twenty-two languages in hardback alone. The artist on the book, Jeff Anderson, who previously worked on Judge Anderson for *2000 AD*, must have been reading the script very carefully, as he is currently in theological college, training to be a vicar. Together with *Doctor Who* TV series writer and novelist Paul Cornell, Mike co-wrote the Big Finish *Doctor Who* audio play *Circular Time*, starring Peter Davison, David Warner and Hugh Fraser. He has had other comic strips published here and there, and is still mostly proud of being responsible for accidentally putting full frontal male nudity in a *Roy of the Rovers* comic strip. *Dreams of Inan: The Worm That Wasn't* is his first novel.

Abaddon Books

Now read a chapter from the first book in
Abaddon's brand new fantasy series,
Twilight of Kerberos...

TWILIGHT of KERBEROS

SHADOW MAGE

MATTHEW SPRANGE

A LUCIUS KANE ADVENTURE

£6.99/$7.99

ISBN: 978-1-905437-54-2

WWW.ABADDONBOOKS.COM

PROLOGUE

Shouts for his blood echoed off the walls of the narrow alley, the worn buildings bouncing the sound so it seemed as though he were surrounded. Casting an anxious glance over his shoulder, he saw nothing through the shadowy gloom and guessed they were still on the street behind.

Not wanting to push his luck, he ran faster, legs straining under the effort and ankles aching from the unfamiliar exertion. A shape shuffled from the darkness of a doorway to his left. e nearly screamed in panic, thinking the murderers behind had caught up with him. The grey-haired beggar gave him a curious look, perhaps wondering why a wild-eyed man was in this region of the city at so late an hour, then shuffled back into his temporary home.

The alley jinked crookedly and, rounding the last corner, he saw the expanse of Meridian Street opening up before him. He slowed down, trying to control his breathing and appear normal, lest he draw attention from revellers or some of the less desirable types he knew frequented the thoroughfare. Drawing his hood up, he wrapped his cloak about him and continued north at a measured pace. The shouts were gradually receding and he began to give a silent prayer of relief. While the events of the evening had been painful, even irreversible, there was still a chance that something could be salvaged from the disaster.

Meridian Street was lit only by the torches and lanterns of the taverns, clubs and brothels that choked its wide midway stretch as it reached, arrow straight, to Turnitia's northern gate. Even those lights were slowly being doused as all but the most stubborn establishments, or those most patronised, depending on how you looked at it, began to call an end to the evening's trade. Only the pale blue giant overhead continued to provide an eerie grey illumination, its cloud strewn surface leering down on the city as the sphere dominated three quarters of the night sky.

He hoped his ancestors, soaring high in the clouds of Kerberos above, were watching over him now, providing whatever aid and protection the true God permitted. Discretely, he made the sign of the Brotherhood under his cloak, and then hurried north. Hoping to appear like a young party-goer finding his way home, but fearing he appeared more like an old man on the run.

Few others were on the street, and even fewer paid him more than a scant glance, having the delights of heavy drink and loose women on their minds. For this, at least, he was grateful, for he could not afford any sort of confrontation, not tonight. The Faith had eyes everywhere, it seemed, and it might not take them long to arrive here if some sort of altercation broke out.

Crossing the cobbled road to avoid two young men obviously, and loudly, looking for a tavern that was still serving new arrivals, he strode purposefully onwards, eventually reaching the point where Meridian Street narrowed. A few closed shop fronts marked the undeclared barrier between entertainment and residential district, and he stopped for a few seconds, watching the road behind to see if any furtive shapes broke from the shadows to continue pursuit. Seeing nothing, he released the breath he had unconsciously been holding, though he knew he would not feel completely safe until he reached home. Perhaps not even then – that, however, was something to deal with in the morning. If he could just survive this night...

He continued his frightened trek and, a few hundred yards further along the road, he turned into a side street he had come to know well. Another turn and he was in the alleys that ran behind the row of close knit dwellings, the simple two storey town houses of a type that sheltered the majority of the inhabitants of the city. Such humble accommodations were perhaps surprising for the man he was to call on, but he had learned they were entirely fitting for the Preacher's outlook on life. In Pontaine, the man would have been revered as a bishop, at the very least, but here, in subjugated Turnitia, the Faith and its lackeys in the Empire of Vos had ensured even this great man remain hidden.

Pausing once again to make sure he was not being followed, ears straining to hear soft footfalls in the twilight, he quietly entered the shadows cast by one house, and tapped on its back door, flecks of paint breaking loose from its ragged surface. Three taps followed by a pause, then two more.

A middle-aged woman opened the door, peering anxiously past him into the alley before focussing on his face. He could sense the fear emanating from her as she hustled him in quickly but that did little to stifle his own relief at, finally, reaching safe territory.

Inside, the kitchen was small and the same as every other house in the street. A small cast-iron stove sitting under the chimney flooded the room with warmth, the fires behind its latticed grate combining with the lantern on the central dark wood table to provide a homely atmosphere, something he was glad of. The man seated at the table grabbed a bottle and poured a generous amount of wine into a clay cup.

"Tabius," the man nodded in welcome. "You look as if you could use this."

"Preacher," Tabius acknowledged. "We should get you to safety. The Faith could have discovered your location by now. They have taken enough of us tonight."

The Preacher waved his concern aside. "I did not run when the Empire descended on our city, even though we all knew they would bring the Final Faith with them. I am not going to start now. Have a drink man, steady your nerves. We don't believe it breaks the divine connection between man and God."

"I heard the Anointed Lord had passed that law," Tabius said, finally accepting the cup and relishing the first sip as it warmed his throat and stomach. "Think her followers will accept it?"

"They had better, if they know what is good for them," the Preacher said then, with a wry smile added, "Whether the Anointed Lord and her closest cronies follow it too, ah, that would be the question. Still, what can you expect when women are allowed into religion? Now, sit, and tell me how we fare this evening."

Tabius sat across from the Preacher and smiled in thanks as his wife laid out a plate of bread and ham, though he did not touch the supper, instead cradling the cup of wine in his hands to warm it.

"They knew where we were and what we were doing," he began, wincing slightly as the screams of dying friends echoed in his ears once again. "Someone gave us up. Tanner, maybe. He was a little too ready to offer us his cellar, knowing the risks it carried."

The Preacher shook his head. "I find that difficult to believe. I have known Tanner a long time, and would declare him righteous. He accepted the risks because he knew they were necessary. However, we have taken in new believers recently, and who knows whether they are all truly genuine? Even with recommendations, it is within some men to only deceive."

"Truly. The Rites of Protection and Good Health had barely finished when the Faith arrived. They were among us before we knew it, striking with swords at anyone within reach. Not just the men – they were after everyone."

He stopped to take another sip of wine, hoping the motion would conceal the shaking he felt enter his hands. The compassion in the Preacher's eyes told him he had failed, and he took a deep breath before continuing.

"It was complete chaos. People were running in all directions, trying to get out. And the screaming. It filled the cellar. We were slipping on the blood running across the floor, men were struck down as they tried to help their wounded sons. Gregor rallied first and began to fight back – I remember a hammer in his hand. We followed him as he headed for the stairs. I saw him cut down, but some of us, I don't know, maybe a dozen, managed to get out. Once we were on the street, we just ran."

"And you were chased."

"Yes. We split up. I don't know if the others escaped. I was hoping I would find some of them here, as I went all the way round the Five Markets before coming back towards Meridian Street. I know Sanser, Mikels and Dornire got out with me, and I think I saw Kurn as well."

"Did the guard not come?"

"I saw a couple but..." Tabius paused. "The thing is I could have sworn they were in on it. Or, at least, some of them were. Since the city fell, the guard step in if you so much as knock a barrel over in the market. They must have seen what was happening, they just had to – but I did not see any of them act."

The Preacher nodded. "We have no friends in the Empire of Vos, and the Faith is fast taking root in the highest levels of their leadership. This Katherine may be a woman but as Anointed Lord, she has garnered a great deal of support among the Lord Dukes. I shudder to think what favours she has granted them, but her power is undeniable. Even here, in Turnitia, we feel the weight of her growing authority. We will find no justice from the city guard."

He reached across the table to top up Tabius' cup, though it had barely been touched. Tabius took this as a sign to drink, and he dutifully raised the cup to his lips.

"Gregor gone, you say? He will be missed in this hour of need." The Preacher sighed as he watched his wife fussing over the stove. "Aldene wants us to pack up and head for Pontaine. Perhaps even Allantia, she says. The Brotherhood is welcome there, she believes, or is at least not persecuted."

This caused his wife to glance over her shoulder with a reproachful look at her husband, and he smiled fondly back at her. Tabius shifted uneasily as he witnessed the love between them speak silent volumes.

"Perhaps that would be for the best," he ventured.

The Preacher hooted at that. "Would you?" he asked. "Really? Leave behind everything you have built up here for a new life? The grass is always greener, as they say but, in truth, you have sweated and worked too hard to build your little empire here. I have worked just as hard, my boy. While you have amassed a small fortune in gold with your warehouses, I have become just as rich in spirit, bringing new blood into the Brotherhood and guiding those who believe to the best of my ability."

He fell silent for a moment, and Tabius stared into his cup. "No," the Preacher finally said. "I will stay and do what must be done. Our people will be scared after tonight, and will need reminding that the trials God puts before us are necessary for the salvation of all of us. Yes, even those poor misguided fools of the Faith. They have their part to play in his grand design too."

"So, what do we do now?" Tabius asked. Though he knew, come morning, a thousand problems would be waiting for him in his growing business. The Preacher had a knack of inspiring him to always work that little bit harder for the Brotherhood. His money and connections among the merchants of Turnitia had already benefited their congregation. All the Preacher had to do was ask, and he would serve as best he could.

"We start again," the Preacher said confidently. "Our beliefs are strong enough to survive the cruelty of the Final Faith. No matter how many of us they threaten, bully or kill, you cannot stamp out the truth my boy. And truth is on our side. They have twisted the word of God beyond all recognition, turning it into a dream of conquest. But that is all it can be – a dream. We carry the burden of God's will Tabius, and so we cannot fail. Whatever the tests put before us, we are God's chosen. Take comfort in that."

"As you say, Preacher."

"Now, come morning we will have a clearer idea of what our losses were. We will need a new meeting place – you can help with that, I trust?"

Tabius thought hard. Though one of his many warehouses by the docks would be a perfect venue for their gatherings, they had avoided it up to now, as it had seemed too dangerous with agents of the Final Faith constantly looking for signs of the Brotherhood growing in the city. Still, he had several that were away from the main trading areas, and his own name was nowhere near their legal documents of possession.

"It may be possible, yes," he said slowly, still thinking. "I'll start making arrangements tomorrow. I might be able to have something ready by evening."

"Please make sure you do. I must address our people by then at the latest. They will be terrified and in need of guidance. Perhaps just in need of assurance that everything will turn out the way it should." He smiled.

"One thing is for sure, though. If we can –"

A loud crash of splintering wood resounded in the tiny kitchen. Tabius jerked in shock, looking past the Preacher to where the sound had come from.

"They're here!" cried the Preacher's wife, and she raced across to her husband to put a hand on his shoulder.

The Preacher looked at Tabius. "Go," he said simply.

Tabius stood immediately, as much out of habit of doing whatever the Preacher told him to do. Only then did he hesitate, looking into the man's eyes. He opened his mouth to speak, but the Preacher cut him off.

"Go! Quickly, while you still have time!"

Another crash, this time followed by a triumphant cry, and there were heavy footsteps in the hall outside the kitchen. Panic took over, and Tabius bolted through the back door, leaving the warm kitchen, the Preacher, and his wife behind. He heard shouts and a scream cut short.

Outside, a cry went up from a shadow in the alley to his right, and he dashed blindly left. Stumbling past houses on either side, he heard heavy footsteps with the chink of mail following, and fear gave him extra speed.

Behind, someone called out. "By the law of Vos – halt!"

That only served to drive Tabius on. A gap between houses to his left beckoned, and he dove into the darkness, crashing into a barrow that had been left casually propped up against one of the walls. The noise of man and barrow crashing onto the cobbles seemed deafening to him, and he scrabbled to his feet, ignoring the sting of grazed palms and shins as he burst out into another small street. Looking to each side, he ploughed forward into another alley that ran behind the next row of houses, changing direction to head back to Meridian Street.

Breathless after several minutes of fear-filled flight, he stopped, leaning against an abandoned cart outside a provisions store. He had not noticed that his pursuers had been outpaced, no doubt weighed down by their armour and weaponry. Behind, he saw an orange glow silhouetting the city's skyline, and he strained his ears to hear massed cries in the distance. Smoke rose in columns from fires near the centre of Turnitia to lazily float in a growing cloud across the face of Kerberos, the massive sphere uncaring and unchanging in the face of human misery, even on this scale. The city, he saw, was descending into riotous chaos, and fellow members of the Brotherhood, people he knew, were the target of the mob, whipped into a frenzy by the Faith.

Slowly, his mind tried to come to terms with what was happening, but the implications of the city guard openly helping the Faith to track down their rivals – or dangerous heretics, as the Brotherhood was no doubt being described – filled him with a sick, creeping dread.

Had he been recognised at the Preacher's house? Tabius thought not, his escape had been too quick, and there had been no time to see his face clearly. Then he thought of the Preacher, and what he might be forced to tell his captors. If, indeed, the man was still alive.

Though weary, he pulled himself up straight and, doing his best to ignore the riots claiming the roads, markets and homes of the city, he carried on up Meridian Street until the north gate came into view. Taking the road that ran behind the city's fortified ramparts, he turned east until the tightly packed houses gave way to much larger dwellings, with their own gardens and protective walls hiding their grounds. This district was known intimately to Tabius. It was home.

Even through his fear, despair and fatigue, he possessed enough awareness to circle his own property twice, staring into the shadows for any sign of movement or presence of the guard. There was nothing, and he guessed the guard would not permit the riots to extend to this part of Turnitia, as there were too many men of power and money living here. Such men rarely entangled themselves in religious conflicts and, living here high on the hill on which Tunisia's foundations were built, they demanded nothing less than a total separation of themselves from the common rabble.

Gingerly opening a small wooden gate in the side wall of his home's compound, he silently slipped in and, closing it behind him, he breathed a heartfelt sigh of release. For the first time that night, he was truly safe. He opened his eyes and looked at his home, a large and finely built town house that took enough space to build perhaps six or seven dwellings of the type the Preacher lived in. Light radiated out from several of the downstairs rooms, and Tabius suddenly yearned to see his family, to make sure they were still safe, even though he knew no harm would touch them here.

His wife whirled round as he entered. Standing in front of the roaring fireplace in the drawing room, he guessed she had been pacing fretfully until he returned. With a cry of relief, she ran into his arms and, for a moment, they just held one another.

"Arthur came by earlier," she said once tears had been choked back. "He said the whole city has turned against you."

Tabius hushed her. "We will be safe. The mob won't climb the hill. There are too many interests to protect here. For once Vos might actually help us, however unintentionally."

"I hope you are right. Arthur said –"

Tabius held his wife at arms length and smiled reassuringly. "While I appreciate Arthur looking after my family while I am away, he is an old man, and I really must have a word to him about scaring you unnecessarily."

"He said people were being killed in the streets. And the fires, I saw them from the landing. Half the city is aflame..."

"It is not as bad as all that. Where are the children?"

"Maggy is asleep. Lucius is pretending to be. He wanted to go down into the city to find his father."

Tabius grinned at that. "Thank God you convinced him otherwise. Now, I have a great deal of work tomorrow. Let's have supper and get some rest. Everything will seem better in the morning, I promise."

She wiped a tear away and nodded. "I'll rouse the kitchen."

Leaving Tabius' side, she walked proudly away, causing him to admire her fortitude, not for the first time. She paused at the door, then turned round. "Tabius... do you hear that?"

Straining his ears, he listened hard, not sure what his wife was getting at. Then it suddenly hit him – the mob was ascending the hill. He could hear their cries, muffled and distant now but slowly growing stronger.

"Impossible," he muttered. "The guard would not dare let them loose. Not up here."

His wife rested on the door handle for support. "Tabius," she said, worry and strain evident in her voice. "Are you sure about that? Really sure?"

One glance at his wife, standing by the door, strong in her faith but unsure of what to do, convinced him.

"Get the children. Do it now!"

As his wife fled upstairs, Tabius crossed the hall to his study, striding to the unlit fireplace to unbuckle the sword that hung there. Though it had belonged to his father and the blade had not been drawn in anger in decades, the lessons hammered into him during adolescence began to flood back as he grasped the hilt and drew the weapon. He fervently hoped he would not have to use it, especially in front of his children, but he would not permit anyone to hurt his family.

Striding back into the hall, he saw his wife leading little Magallia down the stairs, still in her night clothes and rubbing sleep from her eyes. Behind them was Lucius, his pride, about to enter adulthood and take on the responsibilities of the family business. Spying the sword, Lucius had just one question.

"Are we fighting them, Father?"

"I sincerely hope not," Tabius said, though he could not fully suppress a smile at his son's spirit.

A rap at the main door of the house caused them to freeze instantly, before they heard it followed by several more. Three raps, then a pause, followed by two more.

Tabius looked at his wife as he went for the door. "Arthur."

Unbolting the door, he opened it a crack at first, then threw it open when his suspicion was confirmed. Arthur, a stooped man in his seventies but with all the energy of someone far younger, shuffled in.

"You are preparing to leave?" he asked.

"Right now," Tabius said. "I'm not taking any chances. Have you seen anything?"

Turning to gather his family, Tabius stopped when he realised Arthur had not answered. He looked at the old man, and saw tears in the familiar face.

"The guard are already outside," Arthur said. "They are funnelling the mob straight here, avoiding everyone else. When they let me through their line, they said they were happy to let me burn with the rest of you."

Tabius sagged against the door, trying to think furiously what to do. His first thought was for the children. He walked slowly to his wife and took her hand.

"Get the children into the cellar. They will be after the three of us, not the children. They may be... missed in the confusion."

She put a hand on his cheek, and his heart broke at the look of anguish on her face.

"Tabius..." she said, searching for the words. He had nothing of comfort to tell her.

"It is too late."

AVAILABLE AT ALL GOOD
BOOK STORES NOW!